Silver Screen Reflections: Writings on Film

ARROYO SECO PRESS

Edited by Kareem Tayyar

Arroyo Seco Press
www.arroyosecopress.org

Logo by Morgan G Robles
morganrobles.carbonmade.com

Many thanks to Jeffrey Douglas, Keisha Cosand, and Kelly Moffett, without whom this book would not have been possible.

Cover art: *shaunl* from iStock & *Noel_Bauza* from pixabay

ISBN 13: 9781732691186
ISBN 10: 1732691185

This book is dedicated to the memory of Clifton Snider, beloved poet, teacher, colleague, and friend.

Silver Screen Reflections: Writings on Film

ii

Introduction

I know this is usually where the editor writes an extensive introduction that contextualizes the project, and argues for why this particular book, at this particular moment, feels especially vital. But the truth is this collection is based on an idea too simple—and too enduring—to necessitate anything more than the following: movies are awesome. That's been true for over a century, and my guess is it will still be true a century from now.

Without further ado, then, enjoy this book, and enjoy these writers.

—**Kareem Tayyar**, Southern California, September, 2023

Poems

Jeff Alfier

The Collective, 1950
      after Marina Razbezhkina's *Harvest Time*

She jumps from the combine
as if it were burning, runs
through windrows to a crying child,
sucks a thorn from his foot,
washes him in ravine runoff.

Her husband, legless from the war,
watercolors her in a bright green
scarf—a gift for the rescue.

Harvests are white as homespun
wheat on the threshing floor,
light cut by dust motes,

as butterflies that sift the fields,
get stranded in bedrooms at night
like pieces of torn sleeves.

Like the white horse
she must have dreamed.

Tobi Alfier

While Watching *The Lovers on the Bridge* (1991)

They watch the French movie with subtitles.
She eats ice cream, drops her eyes
during quiet parts to attend her spoon.
He eats fennel like an apple, leans
over to give her a licorice kiss.
They are both diverted from the screen
with pleasure, miss the lovers whisper
as they plan a trip to the sea. They
understand it anyway, and next
morning they themselves go to the ocean
and stand on the bluff. With arms
wrapped around waists they lift
their faces to the newborn sun,
seductive as the breath always with
them, their laughter the beautiful
map of anywhere else.

Joan Bauer

Vittorio Gassman in Los Angeles, 1984

She was a photographer for an Italian journal
that wanted portraits of him from the LA tour.
She'd heard about his turbulent marriage,

his Hollywood misadventures playing
the 'Latin lover' roles he despised & how
he'd gone back to Rome, immersed himself

in Italian cinema, created a theatre company,
toured the country, performed Shakespeare,
Dostoevsky & Aeschylus, bringing along

a portable stage. She'd seen *Il Sorpasso* (1962).
Gassman plays Bruno, a rakish man-child,
barreling his Lancia Aurelia convertible down

Rome's empty streets, blasting its offbeat horn.
Mid-August. A holiday! Bruno persuades Roberto,
a naïve law student, (Jean-Louis Trintignant)

to come along. Boisterous adventure, then a turn.
Gassman's incomparable face & movement,
bellisimo longshots of Rome & the surround.

In private, Gassman wasn't boisterous. An introvert.
When she read about his death, she had to sit down.
There'd been decades of depression. He'd said:

'An actor has to be a clown.' Years before,
she'd had questions, but hadn't asked, warned off
by a sadness in his eyes, the armor of his charm.

On the Making of *The Godfather*

The grandfather, the patriarch was known
as *Zumbalcone,* one who jumped from balcony
to balcony, a ladies' man.

He'd say: *Follow your path.*
Never lose the music within you.
His son would become a composer.

The grandson, the director, was only 29
& had been reluctant to take on the potboiler.
But he needed the money & after he scraped

aside the trashier subplots, Coppola saw
a real story about family. He cut up
Mario Puzo's novel, pasted scenes

into a notebook, like a storyboard,
then began writing. He moved the action
to post World War II, insisted on filming

in New York City & a picturesque hilltop
village near Mt Etna. True that Coppola
faked a seizure when the producer resisted

hiring Brando. True that Brando eased
into character by stuffing his cheeks with
Kleenex so he'd look more like a bulldog.

True that Coppola hired Pacino because
the guy 'had the map of Sicily on his face.'
The betrayal & shoot-out scenes iconic.

What I remember: the pregnant Connie
cowering behind a curtain as her husband
beats her. The aged Vito play-growling

a monster, frightening his grandson
with fangs from an orange rind. Fallen
among the tall-stalked tomato vines.

Charlie Brice

The African Queen

I hear the chuff of a boat engine
and wonder if Bogey will save
Katharine Hepburn from the Nazis.
That engine competed with Bogey's
bowel sounds, the grinding gurgle
of his coffee maker, and the drum
in life's jungle.

Kate was such a sweet prude
in that movie; as pure and naïve
as we all are when we start out.
We divide and divide until
we reach our most common denominator,
the remainder that becomes who we are:

The crude and smelly Bogey-alcoholic,
who knows best how to survive, or
take to the cloth, like Kate's brother
in the movie, commune with the Sky Daddy
who's numbered our days and counts the hairs
on our heads (and I thought counting pie tins
at inventory time at my mother's restaurant
supply business was boring). We will,
of course, ignore Jim Harrison's question,
"If the afterlife is so wonderful why did Jesus
bother bringing Lazarus back from the dead?" [1]

[1] Jim Harrison, *The Beast God Forgot to Invent*, Grove Press, 2001.

Maybe we garner a blessing here
or there, settle, get along like Kate,
follow our feelings, respect elders
and tradition, love what we can,
become a soul-force that endures,
persists—knows how to sing a hymn
over a friend, how to make
death less lonely.

Cowbell

I was in my teens before I realized that a cowbell originally dangled
from the neck of an actual cow. Did I finally encounter a cow
with its mini-gong swaying under its rawhide neck, or did
I see one in a John Wayne or Gabby Haze movie, or on one
of the ubiquitous cowboy TV series of childhood:
Roy Rogers, Sky King, Gene Autry?

Before my enlightenment a cowbell was, to me, the obnoxious tinny rattle
that some athlete's mother brought to one of our football games
and shook whenever our quarterback, Mike Barrett, hit Ace Evans
with one of his infrequently completed bombs during the perpetual
losing seasons endured by the St. Mary's Gales in Cheyenne.

I put cowbells in the same category as other irritating noisemakers like those
straw horns that made awful noises as they unraveled when you blew through
them at some miscreant's birthday party or that goofy thing you'd spin that
sounded like a ratchet.

A cowbell came mounted on my first gold spackled cheap Japanese drum kit.
There wasn't much of a place for the cowbell in sixties rock but I played it
on *You Can't Do That* by The Beatles and *Honky Tonk Women* by the Stones—
never connecting it with anything but an outdated prop that added rhythm to a song.

I was a callow city boy far removed from the truth of what gave me milk,
what trod on the dust of dairy farms, and the white health squirted into pails
eventually transformed into cream and butter.

We are held hostage by our upbringing and the lacunae it inevitably creates.
A cowbell clanged of dung, dun, and dirty callused hands—what high school
football, asphalt, and amplifiers took for granted and left behind.

Kelsey Bryan-Zwick

Date Nights

We watch every movie
Tom Waits has cameoed in
also, Kurt Vonnegut

We watch Kung Fu movies
everything with Bruce Lee
and between these, discs that arrive
sporadically in the mail
from your late-night insomnia research
the screen of your face
aglow in blue light

Your love of Stephen King
and *One Flew Over the Cuckoo's Nest*
caroms in your gushing, analysis of
characters spills from your lips

We both agree the new *Star Wars*
and anything by Disney
is overrated

We laugh loudly at *Borat*
and make lists of all the films
we still want to watch together

Anders Carson

Mosquito glory at dusk

Children are swinging on the swings
beneath the peeling screen.
Pajama town as they run around playing tag.
Rusted minivans come in and are asked
to park at the back
beside pick-up trucks and RV's.
There is courtesy in the parking
everyone getting a chance
to *see.*
Mesh tents, and weaved orange and green lawn chairs
from the 70's
have appeared.
Mosquito mesh and green electrical tape
plugging rolled down windows
like some Southern Nascar race car.
You want to keep them out
before the damage is done.
There is a line-up at the concession stand.
Snow cones, popcorn and candy that sends moviegoers
into sweet salted bliss.
There is the soft smell of marijuana that clouds the screen
as Woody the Woodpecker dances his zaniness
and the children look up and scatter back to their people.

It's a triple feature tonight.
A soft, sedated family film
followed by a romantic comedy
and then deep into the darkness
chainsaws are fired up,
blood flows, expletives mount
and clothing edges to the floor.

After each film there is a fogger who goes by in a suit
to deal with the mosquitoes.
It puffs out magic clouds and gets embedded
in your hair and skin.
Those winged creatures stop biting
for a little while
but their hunger is persistent and
the evening bacchanal of sucking blood
begins again.

Windshield steams up from close caressing
and playful persistent fondling.
The moon rises.
Last call for treats
as the summer night lasts forever
laughter, trained nostalgia of honking at vehicles
who've turned on their lights.
It's on evenings like this that the plotting is finalized.
You will be able to leave and start again.
Tobacco inhaled from some yogic release
followed by a candid cough.
Getting away from the agonizing day
screen darkens
giant drive-in reels,
no longer turning.

Kimberly Esslinger

At the Drive In

We sit watching the big screen under the fattest moon
eating popcorn like it was our first meal in a hundred days
wrapped in our little cocoon of metal and machine
separated from all the dramas and comedies
of strangers fucking and fighting around us—
windows open, weed drifting in
and I'm happy
that you're happy
we have no time for urgent hero stories
battling every day against the ticking clock
saving women, saving children, saving mothers,
saving kittens, theoretically saving ourselves
and all this saving makes us weary
as I grab your hand to fly away and
use our superhero powers to stay awake.

City Limits
after *The Last Picture Show*

Making out in the back seat
with your girl but the girl
you want is in the front seat
with your best friend,
and he's crazy
in love with her—
the prettiest girl in town
and everyone knows but
no one ever says
her mother is prettier.
Love goes to the loser.
This is gospel according to Ruth
the football widow
who gives herself to you
in her sad tired bed.
Squeaking, squeaking.
Gives you her plain, small
body. Itchy at forty the way
some men need a fast car
or just need new. She hopes
you see her. Wants you
to value her, but she knows
that's too much. Jesus said
all women are Mary,
but maybe all women are Ruth
or Jayce, or maybe a Lois,
fenced in by nowhere else to go
and the days sprawl for miles.

Edward Field

The Return of Frankenstein

He didn't die in the whirlpool by the mill
where he had fallen in after a wild chase
by all the people of the town.

Somehow he clung to an overhanging rock
until the villagers went away.

And when he came out, he was changed forever,
that soft heart of his had hardened
and he really was a monster now.

He was out to pay them back,
to throw the lie of brotherly love
in their white Christian teeth.

Wasn't his flesh human flesh
even made from the bodies of criminals,
the worst the Baron could find?

But love is not necessarily implicit in human flesh:
Their hatred was now his hatred,

so he set out on his new career
his previous one being the victim,
the good man who suffers.

Now no longer the hunted but the hunter
he was in charge of his destiny
and knew how to be cold and clever,

15

preserving barely a spark of memory
for the old blind musician
who once took him in and offered brotherhood.

His idea—if his career now had an idea—
was to kill them all,
keep them in terror anyway,
let them feel hunted.
Then perhaps they would look at others
with a little pity and love.

Only a suffering people have any virtue.

Celeste Gainey

best boy

The chief assistant to the gaffer on a movie or television set. There are no "best girls" per se.
—IMDB Glossary

At the age of three
I tell my mother:

When I grow up, I'm going to be a man.
Like Pancho in *The Cisco Kid*:
high-heeled boots, a six-shooter.
Halloween, I'm a pirate with a hook,
in the Christmas pageant I insist on the Nutcracker
or Mouse King, never Marie.

Either grade, girls talk:
Who will get married? Make a good mother?
Not one can see me as a wife with kids.
It hurts a little to hear I'm not like them.
I'm a boy in a kilt and knee socks—
When I grow up, I'm going to play the field.

In high school I meet a boy
I either love or want to be.
He wears madras shirts, crosses his legs elegantly,
holds his Winston like a lady.
One day in a crowded elevator as a joke
he yells *Fuck, fuck, fuck!*
All you ever want to do is fuck! Who do you think I am—
Superman?
No, I say, I'm Superman!
You're Lois Lane.

Just out of film school,
I apply for membership in the Union.
All the Local 52 boss wants to know —
can I carry *horsecock* same as any man?
All I want to know — will he let me join his band of brothers,
be Best Boy — apprentice
to Vinnie Delaney, Milty Moshlak,
Dusty Wallace, Dickie Quinlan:
set their spider-boxes, haul their 4-aught,
flag their barn-doors, trim their brute arcs,
run their stingers, scrim their broads,
wrap their 9-light fays;
let them make me a man.

dog day afternoon

(1975, Sidney Lumet, dir.)

Medium shot:
NYPD blue & white pulls up,

Leon, Sonny's trans lover, emerges
from the back—gaunt, matted fro,

flimsy hospital robe, tired mascara
racooning his eyes.

Take after take
the door flings open, its window flares.

no matter which way/
how many times I tweak the flag on the fill.

I feel a hand on my shoulder.
I turn to find Mr. Lumet

at full attention.
What's the problem?

I start to explain,
He raises his hand.

I'll cut before that, he says.
Don't worry about it.

Then looking into me,
It doesn't matter.

between takes

Taxi Driver (1976, Martin Scorsese, dir.)
Columbus Circle, summer 1975

De Niro idles in his Checker. Cybill flirts behind
her Jackie-Os. Scorsese sucks oxygen from a tiny
tank trailed by an assistant. Albert Brooks hogs
the PA: *When using the moving sidewalk,*
please stand to the right, if you wish to pass, please
do so on the left. Over & over. Grips lay dolly track
for a shot we all know will never make the final cut
but will take most of the day to shoot.
Me in my 501s & Mighty Mouse T-shirt,
20 feet up, work gloves & pliers protruding,
the brute arc light I tend sputters & hisses
beside me. Like that famous *New Yorker* cover
showing the world as seen from 9th avenue—
the land of make believe rises up
to swallow me whole.
I try to lean as if belonging against
the unsteady rungs of my ladder—oblivious
to the real world down there too—
passing me by; most, jaded New Yorkers,
their eyes on the prize, but maybe some
looking up & wondering *what's that girl doing*
up there in the sky—flying so close to the sun?
Some kind of myth. With pliers

god bless susan tyrrell

Fat City (1972, John Huston, dir.)

Oma, the unzipped sherry-loving lush at the end of the bar in Huston's *Fat City*,
slurring, *do you know who your friends are?* Half-falling into the arms of Keach's
you can count on me Billy Tully, has-been boxer; Conrad Hall's
moth-pocked light slanting in high
and honeyed, dust showers and beatific shine cloaking the two dreamers
in this Loserville of late
afternoon San Joaquin Valley, 1972. Days talking gibberish on a bar stool,
nights ranting in a rented room. Forgiveness, if not redemption,
somewhere last down the road.
At the Oscars that year, Sacheen Littlefeather,
former *Miss American Vampire*, refuses Best Actor
for the protesting Godfather, Marlon Brando, then becomes a *Playboy* centerfold;
Keach doesn't even get a nod. Tyrrell gets nominated as Best Supporting
but doesn't win; Eileen Heckert does, for *Butterflies Are Free*—forgotten now.
You're the only son-of-a-bitch worth shit in this place, Oma tells Tully, *these others,*
I wouldn't ask 'em the time of day.

George Hammons

Nebula

Of all the Marvel characters
it is Nebula with whom I most relate
tested, deconstructed, then reassembled,
by her father
who sees her weaknesses
as justifications
for his cruelties

When I was small my father once
leaned close to my face and
shouted
"What the fuck is wrong with you
you're always standing around like somebody
did something to you?"

So, like Nebula,
I said nothing and
waited for the shattered pieces
to reassemble themselves
into something he could love.

Brian Harman

80s Movies

I was Brat Pack age in a Brat Pack era
in the luster of blockbuster beginnings,
when the rain was purple and dancing
turned dirty,
when sixteen candles was a risky business
in white briefs, cruising across the floor
in white crew socks,
when the only princess bride I wanted
was a weird science experiment
in lipstick and panties,
when the darkside of poetry
was a cloaked father and Gotham justice,
when breakfast club society was stuck in
detention with dead white poets
and the existential nothing neverending,
when sunglasses disguised a weekend
or decoded signs and aliens,
when a song was sung about not being
afraid of no ghost except
when the TV went static,
when the known don'ts were don't fall
asleep, don't feed them after midnight,
don't say his name three times,
when waxing on and off and painting
the fence was not a summer job,
when phoning home was finding a dime
in a pocket next to
some chocolate peanut butter pieces,
when nerd revenge got bush inception,
when bacon loosened up a small town,
when a banana in a tailpipe stopped

two cops and an expired Twinkie saved
one from die hard hunger,
when instead of planes or trains,
they should have taken the Delorean to
Thanksgiving,
when Bueller, Bueller, anybody,
when snakes were hated and a goose
was a companion to talk to,
when a cyborg assassin had a muscular
Austrian accent,
when a held-up boombox was a symbol
of in-your-eyes love,
when she was pretty in fuchsia,
wore blue neon velvet, faked an orgasm
at a restaurant, cargo-bayed an egg-laying
bitch into outer space,
when the right thing was the right stuff.

Moby Dick (1956), Born Free (1966)

The VHS double feature rented for me
when I lived with my dad in my early 20s
in the mid-90s, when I was stuck in bed
in a full leg cast—it was the only thing
I can remember him really doing for me
during the four weeks of immobility.
No cup of water, no easy to reach popcorn
or snacks, just the two old-ass film classics.
He selected the movies, not because I asked;
I didn't ask him for anything. But I did end
up watching them as they had to be returned
in two days, and I had to be kind and rewind.
That was the video store policy back then.
All I can recall is—I was in and out of sleep,
Gregory Peck looked like Abraham Lincoln
with a harpoon on an obsessed voyage on
the rock-sway ocean on a whaling ship—
the Pequod, and the ball of my foot was
on fire from the coarse edge of the plaster
of Paris cutting into my skin. I took a Vicodin
only once to test it. It didn't help. I don't recall
what happened to Captain Ahab or the whale.
I never read the book. From what I remember—
Born Free was a British movie about a family
caring for an orphaned lion; based on a true
story. The theme song's chorus, sung by
crooner Andy Williams has never left my ear:
Born freeeeeeeeeee, as free as the wind blows...
That's it. I don't know what happened after that.

Maybe my dad empathized with the movies—
he wanted a safe house from his traumatic
upbringing, maybe he felt unresolved, unloved,
maybe he wanted a normal family to take care
of him—maybe he wanted Ahab-style revenge
for his suffering, maybe he related to the whale,
or both. Maybe he wanted me to somehow watch
it be played out. Maybe, I didn't understand.
Maybe, I had my own pain to navigate and mend.

Donna Hilbert

Giulietta Hears a Prophecy

If you hit the road with a white clown
you will beat the drum to announce
his arrival, sleep in a tent,
eat soup from a pail.

Travel with a white clown
and you will play the trumpet
for an order of nuns, be abandoned
at the side of the road, wave
to the world from the back of a wagon.
You will sit by the sea and pray.

Marry the white clown
and you will beat the drum to announce
his arrival, suffer fools in his service
be his lover, his cuckold, his muse.
You will close your eyes
when you sit by the sea and watch
the whole circus world unfurl.

You will bury the white clown
after a marriage of fifty years and one day.
And when you die, a few months later
it will be he who beats the drum
announcing your arrival
into the everlasting circus town.

Guilietta Masina February 22, 1921-March 23,1994

From *The New York Times* obituary:

Guilietta Masina, the waiflike actress who became one of Italy's best-known movie stars, died today in a Rome hospital less than five months after the death of her husband, the director Federico Fellini. She was 73.

Paul Hostovsky

Favorites

"My favorite part of the movie was when
he cut off that guy's head with two swords—
what was yours?" My 8-year-old son
is in PG-13 heaven. His little mug is all lit up
like the moon in love with a marquee
as we spill out of the Framingham-14
cineplex, late already for his mom's,
who will have my head for this
and that. PG-13 for pervasive violence
and some sexual content. My favorite
is his favorite subject, research topic,
science project he's trying to make grow
in a specially reserved corner of my crowded
ear. He waters it with questions while I drive:
"What's your favorite color? food? animal?
movie? part of the movie?" The sad part is
my favorite escapes me like a runaway balloon,
a green one, growing smaller and smaller, a tiny
speck above a childhood in Plainville, New Jersey.
Now it bumps up gently against the windshield
and he bats it at my head. Divorced white male with no
favorites seeks favorite. In my forties,
the wrinkles on my forehead have begun to resemble
an approximately-equal-to sign: Everything
tastes like chicken. Mostly what we're faced with
are these questions concerning the things we don't
love. Because we don't love things. As though
loving people weren't work enough. I tell him
he's my favorite as I pull into his mom's
driveway, her head poking out the front door
like a cuckoo in a perfectly accurate clock.

But he rolls his eyes at my easy wrong answer,
maybe because it's the plain truth and because
the truth is plain: G for generally happy, intact families
in your face like balloons, red-white-and-blue ones,
blocking your view of beauty which is
heads rolling and chariots crashing
and whole civilizations going up in smoke,
not to mention the mothers with their infinitely
varying breasts floating before the green eyes
of the incredibly shrinking fathers in disfavor.

Serena Kamlani

winter in the city of stars

i live in the land of postcard winters
not the sort that's snow-capped and sparkly
but rather the "wish you were here" sort
featuring a sky imprinted with silhouetted palm trees

the dissonance is glaring:
an idyllic, fantasy whirlwind trapped inside a snowglobe
set apart and lit up on a silver screen
and the world outside baking in the december sun
enveloped in a smoggy haze

alone in my snowglobe, suspended above the city
the domed glass walls reduce the sounds of hustle and bustle
to a faint whisper
christmas trees below twinkle in solitude
dressed up for anyone, but nowhere to go

i am as strange to this place as it is to me
cars zoom by in a quiet flash
amidst the occasional muffled horn
as even the dull roar of traffic seems to hiss
"you don't belong here."

William Mohr

At the Global Multiplex

"Do you really want
to see *The Babadook*?"
"A part of me is curious,"
I say. "Which part?" "The look /

don't look" parting of
the red sea of climate change.
The planet is a pop-up book:
glaciers melt, but I don't cringe.

Flip a page and watch the rain
forests spewing brittle kites
of ashes from the haunted stain
of a hundred thousand acres burnt.

Not everyone gets to relax
at this movie for free. I must confer
some distance with my purchased snacks
for Irony, like Nature, to endure.

Labials

for Marilyn Monroe

Letters pronounced by lips:
m, p, b. Your name bounces
a pair of m's, a hum of men
at movies. Your pictures
clipped from magazines
billow like frothing clouds
before a clump of a storm.

The wretchedness of beauty
is they only notice you and not
what your eyes linger on,
an amethyst glass knob
at the end of a gear shift.

Your masseuse fingers your chin.
She's seen a thousand figures
spray up from behind: legs
arching into waists and shoulders
but when they spin around, each face
withers faster than chrysanthemums
in a tall vase. Your glow promises
what any woman, adored,
wants to promise only once.

On a hot summer night, a boat's
anchored to a bobbing slosh.
A reclining man knows which line
was meant for Marilyn—
"I don't feel anything any more."
Isn't that what a woman says
when she yearns to be stunned?
Love should be perfect, but no one is,
until the heart you've won is your own.

Dave Newman

Watching *Full Metal Jacket* With My Grandfather

The marine drill sergeant turns
to Private Pyle and says
"How tall are you, Private Pyle?"

and Private Pyle says
"5 feet, 10 inches tall, sir"

and the drill sergeant says
"I didn't know they stacked
shit that high, Private Pyle"

and I cough a little
to maybe cover the word shit
because my grandfather
does not like profanity

and I am seventeen
and rented the movie
which you were supposed
to be 18 to rent.

I often pretend the world
is not the world
so I can keep living in it.

Private Pyle
fat-faced and slow-witted
clumsy and sloppily dressed
uncomfortably laughs
like he knows
in thoughts
he can barely comprehend

because he's never thought them before
that he will need
to point his gun
at the chest
of the red-face man
shouting words like bullets into the target of his face.

The drill sergeant
played by retired drill sergeant
        Ronald Lee Ermey
a Vietnam Vet and graduate
of the University of Manila
a man who wears a hat like a weapon
and his shirt like a weapon
and boots to stomp
your brains in
will be nominated for a Golden Globe
and the performance is hot as a burning forest
and will scare the brave
right out of any viewer.

The barracks looks like a jail
made of fear and screaming

and after making
Private Pyle choke himself

the drill sergeant says
"What is your major
malfunction, numbnuts?"

and my grandfather says
"Aww now, that language"

and I keep staring at the TV screen
        wondering how
I can turn it off
without looking like
I'd like to keep it on.

My grandfather says "Aww now" a lot
but not as judgement
though of course as judgement
but as a verbal reminder to himself
        to rise above our failings.

It's Sunday and he's back from church
and we're eating the chicken and dumplings
my grandmother made in a pressure cooker.

My grandfather was 33 when he was drafted
        to fight in World War II
one kid at home, one kid on the way.

He left his job as an electrician at the power plant
        where he performed essential work
        the kind of work
        that kept you from war
and headed to boot camp with a bunch
of kids from Pittsburgh and West Virginia
and small towns everywhere.

The US government dropped the bombs
that caused the enemy to surrender
as my grandfather shipped out.

He seldom talked about it, the war or the bombs
        not in a dramatic way

because he moved
through the present
with great enjoyment
and hope for the future.
He believed in Heaven as a reward.
He believed in Jesus Christ as a guide.
He believed in work as the only means
to happiness.

He said "A lot of good boys died
on both sides" if anyone asked

then he finished his biscuit or picked up
his hammer or maybe both simultaneously.
He loved sausage and eggs and remodeling
houses he could flip for extra money.

Nonethless, bombs.

While people who looked nothing
like my grandfather
        turned to fire and ash
everyone in America celebrated

and my grandma thanked God
for keeping her husband safe

and my grandfather's ship
dropped him off on some island
off the coast of mainland Japan

and someone with more stripes
gave my grandfather a job
prepping old Jeeps

to deliver supplies
once the relief effort started

and I have this black-and-white photo of him
          looking handsome in welder gloves
                    blowtorch in hand
                    goggles pulled up
on his head
                    leaning on a Jeep
          and smiling over some scrap metal.

How lucky some of us are
or how blessed
or how strong
or all three in unison
to be able to endure the pain
of existence like bugs yapping
around your face and neck and eyes
and not like the tragedy of being alive.

After Private Pyle kills the drill sergeant
he puts the barrel of the rifle in his mouth
and finds the answer to all his questions.

I'd never seen a war movie like that
          where most of the war
          happens at home
          in boot camp.

Sometimes you find out what you want
to do and what you don't want to do
          at the exact same moment.

I knew I wanted to make art
and not go to war but not how
I was going to do one
and avoid the other.

Such are the choices of working-class boys
everywhere in the world
        whether we know it or not.

If my grandfather would have met Stanley Kubrick
        the man who directed *Full Metal Jacket*
        a man who was never a soldier
        who never did anything really
        but take advantage of the people
who worked with and for him
and make a half dozen fucking fantastic films

my grandfather would have said
"Aw now, Stanley, why'd you make
those boys swear so much?
        Ain't nothing were that bad."

Sarah Perna

The Hollywood Romantics

It's the looks,
You know which looks.
The revelations,
The speeches,
All the stuff of my (day)dreams.

It's Mr. Coulson on the Ferris Wheel,
when we know the truth, but he can't know yet.
Otherwise, we'd never get the payoff of him
running down the steps,
"Don't Worry Baby" playing as Josie
Finally gets kissed.

It's Monica and Quincy playing
one-on-one for love.
And just when we think it's over,
that we somehow got this all wrong,
Quincy says: "double or nothing"

It's how Seb walks with Mia in the Hollywood Hills
to retrieve their cars,
"What a waste of a lovely night…"
It's not - we think, as it's revealed that Seb's car
was parked next to the house,
And not up the winding drive of Mulholland.

It's Samantha spotting Jake Ryan
outside the church,
"Me?" We ask with her,
"Yeah, you"

It's just a girl standing in front of a boy.
It's "In Your Eyes" on Lloyd's boom-box.
And clichéd as it has become,
It's even Jerry declaring "You complete me"

As the music crescendos,
my heart swells.
Inevitably, unavoidably, inescapably
these Hollywood romantics
have ruined me.

Ben Rosenbush

My Cast Iron Pan and I

My cast iron pan says it wants more from our relationship
than frying a morning egg. So, I ask if it wants to take in

a movie. It leans against the couch on its one leg
as we watch an old western. But things feel a bit off

when the cowboys cook with what looks like its kin, and when
another pan gets used to deflect an ambush of bullets.

I carry it around, getting ready for bed, and it stares at me
with that open face looking cold, looking in the direction

of the stove. That night, it cries small, black beads of
grease that stains the pillows

                    and in its dreams, it clinks
against the side of a lost thoroughbred, sauntering through
the dark silver shards of night, under a milky ghost moon
Clint Eastwood shoots dead, blowing smoke out of his gun.

In the morning, I don't ask, and nod to my pot to hard-boil
breakfast. That's when I get the feeling that my cast iron pan

wants to knock me dead. But it only asks to be placed back in the
cupboard, with the rest, neatly stacked in the dark. We haven't

talked in a long time. But I think of it on occasion and wonder
if it thinks about me, about the perfect egg we used to fry,

the loneliness like two lovers filmed in separate
rooms, leaned against the split screen of each other,

before the rom-com has found its way to resolve.

The Parkway Theater

We didn't know what we'd see, though
it didn't matter, on the nights
we'd visit the Parkway—

a wine bottle each in our coats,
a shared bucket of popcorn between us,

almost alone inside the greasy theater
less known for its films than for being
that strange neighbor known

for the best stories, like that time
the whole theater went completely bright white
from a broken reel, the projector light spraying

its total beam across everything, across
us, like blinding visitations of angelic
announcement, revealing that hidden
thing illuminating each scene.

Patty Seyburn

On the Waterfront

Marlon Brando lectures on the subjunctive in the living room,
carried away with the possibility of what could have been had
       things been
different
though no one knows how different they would have to be.
                     Change responds
to increment and earthquake, depending.
The conditional is our favorite state, one with numerous borders
       and lakes,
an attractive bird, flower and motto. In California we have a
       state butterfly with
legions of supporters.
                We must all set our boundaries,
so friends and family tell me
and I tell them back, not out of any debt to echo, though I
       appreciate
the rhetorical effects of repetition—
but, you see, we've only so much time, and we are greedy for each
       others.
               This is the New Greed,
which closely resembles the Old Greed and the Ancient Greed,
though the Prelapsarian Greed's another story.
I never liked Eva Marie Sant; she seems a whiner, and I don't
       understand the inversion in her last name. This film is full of
       those
            kinds of corruptions.

Bell, Book and Candle

My mother looked like Hedy Lamaar
but I've never seen a movie starring Lamaar or Dorothy Lamour
                              for that matter
so let's talk about Kim Novak
who, says my mother, "isn't so great."
                              Sometimes we crave
          the other and sometimes we despise it.
Novak played a gorgeous witch.
We don't imagine witches looking like that—so cool blonde—
because
                              we've adopted
that crazy classical notion that beauty outside
is inside, too. She's what we'd call a "good witch"   someone
with powers
          used mainly to benefit the human race
or her close friends. Jack Lemmon, her warlock brother,
would lift his arms gracefully and turn on the streetlamps, which
I have tried,
                              without success.
Sometimes we don't need success.
They spent time at the bongo club   like poets of yore,
          or myths of poets of yore—when exactly was yore?
We used to have such nice associations:
surface vs. substance, free verse and tennis; now I can't assume
anything.
                              My mother's other
Hollywood wisdom: "Robert Taylor broke
Barbara Stanwyck's heart." It's good to have firm beliefs
          in the quotable
          when pain is at stake.

Faith Shearin

Watching Zombie Movies With Our Daughter

Mavis and I watched Zombie movies that first June
after you died; maybe you saw
us walking through rain

without umbrellas along the avenues of Amherst
where peonies grew so fat they fainted
and children caught fireflies in their cupped hands,

then opened their fingers to flickering light;
we favored a cinema with a triple feature, bought
popcorn and candy, sat at the back

where the seats were broken, behind rows
of strangers in hats, and considered
the undead: their fingers reaching through the silence

of cemeteries, digging their way
back to this world; we watched
zombies return to the neighborhoods

where they once rode bikes and climbed trees
and kissed and dreamed: skin chalky,
arms extended, slack-jawed, stumbling.

Clifton Snider

Brokeback Mountain **(2005)**

Jack and Ennis,
two sheep-herding cowboys,
gaze slyly at each other
before they find themselves
in lust and love
in a tent
on Brokeback Mountain.

Never again will they be
so whole,
so one with themselves
in the chill of the mountain
like the cowboy shirts Jack saves
one inside the other.

Thomas R. Thomas

Science Fiction

Sci fi stories
of the Fifties
ignite

the fertile
imaginings of
a young heart

leaving me
on the beach
and on a

far flung
forbidden planet
on the lookout

for the
invaders from Mars
wary of the

war of the worlds
watching for the day
the Earth stood still

and ever vigilant
for the day a great
blob falls from space

leaving a sparkle in
my eyes each night
lying in my bed

Fiction

Douglas Cole

Persian Night

Angeline was mixing up the medicine from her shelves stacked with mason jars full of herbs and roots and eye of newt. A smile on her face. No sandwich made with hate, here, but a humming lovely music in the background of redbird warm mist as the dream potion bubbled and alchemized under her hands. And as I sat at the counter there, I thought indeed, this is probably a perch he'd held many a full moon night such as this as the balewinds blew and wooed their way through the screens and curtains.

Slinking along comes Morph the cat.

"I'm not sure what I'm hoping to find in these," I said. "But I do enjoy reading them."

I'm selling my soul
and she's charging me interest

"You never know what you'll discover in there," she said. "Sometime I think he just liked to make sounds."
"He write about you?"
"I'm usually the witch-goddess of chaos."

Her pots rattled with steam seeping around the lids, and on her cutting board were little piles of Greenleaf and black seed. She fine-chopped and rubbed the ingredients between her fractionizing hands and then mince-added them layer by layer into her brew.

"What is that you're making?" I said.
She smiled and looked at me with dark enigma eyes. "Some tea," she said.
"Tea, huh?"
"Tea."

Spring

Easter now and a strange night
crossing the line into longer light
the energy source just within reach
like an extended day of the dead
like an Escher hand drawing
a hand drawing itself in
another version of Michelangelo's
God touching the finger of Adam
or Octavio Paz beholding himself
through the Blue Bouquet with
the great eye looking down
through the microscope of sky

"You ready?" she said.
"What'll it do to me?"
"You don't have to be anywhere for a while, do you?"

She placed a cup of the hot elixir on the counter before me. On the surface of the cup little dragonfish swirled around like visual laughter. I felt my stomach tighten and my heart speed up. Here we go...

I'm experienced and have seen and been the cosmic wow...

And the music in the background was electronica motion indigo mind-bath with cascading rhythms descending in chromatic four-chord progressions, a little baroque and reborn and leading to the one and only one conclusion, that there was no disbelief to suspend. Ah, seek nothing, the fool is on the loose! And these were just subtle variations at this point rippling through a more or less preconceiving lizard cortex and maybe sinking down to the sub-cellular level half imagined and half remembered because I was not the first nor the last.

A fly entered the scene with big black heavy-weight buzzing like a military transport plane nearly colliding with my forehead. Now that was intentional! A few moments later

it was gone, but I couldn't stop seeing those green beveled
hair spindle eyes. That was a close one! So I read some more:

I was a hot fever tropical earthquake
land fragment in a stream —
I thought I was in a movie
with good effects and mist parting —

      I continued to read, but I was a little distracted by the
effects or what I imagined were the effects because it might
have just been some blissful sip of the Hippocrene for all I
knew, and the worst thing that was going to happen was that
I would have to go to the bathroom all night. Angeline was
out on the patio with a candle glowing and the liquid
Buddha fountain flowing and the little lights on strings
glittering in the wisteria above her as she played some lovely
tune on the guitar. Was this heaven? Nothing was really
happening. I kept thinking that. Nothing is really happening.
Or it was a question. Was anything happening? I just think it
is. Or, I just think it isn't. Or is it?

The Universal Clown

See, you can call it an office
you can call it a prison cell
you can call it the inside of your skull
and time is an abstract notion
going on somewhere else
while in here find portals
to Guatemala, Paris, LA,
Mount Fuji and New York City
The Five Spot or a grave in the woods
and I go through a plume of ash
commotion of coming and going
and I'd probably stay here forever
if I didn't get bored or know
a little guidance is needed
from time to time even from
a cosmic jester like me.

51

And did I hear out there in the night streets someone singing Old Macdonald Had a Farm, E I E I O? And over that, Angeline's guitar and her humming soft and low...

A lovely glow of light was filling up the room and seemed to flutter and roll rippling with swirling internal eddies and crests and plumes, ah glorious waves, attuned in perfect synchronous frequency with the humming of the refrigerator, I think it was.

The big fly came back around. In my mind I heard Rutger Hauer saying, where are you going?

My hands felt cold.
My feet felt cold.
This was a sign.
But what was coming?

Big fly swung by, and I looked into his eye. And then I read these lines:

The ground is crumbling beneath me
eviction notice fluttering on the door
And the landlord changed the locks

I wanted to ask Angeline about this one, but the effort seemed colossal, and she was in a space of her own. What was he writing about? Was it historical and specific? Metaphoric? Both? Often more than it seemed, the letters themselves took on a life of their own. I was in the handwriting space, you see? Much more intimate there and extreme, sort of like the quantum idea that even in the most solid forms there is more space than substance, unedited, raw, direct. The cold marble under my hands, for example, was once a pretty secure promise, but now it was showing its hem, and I looked down into its tectonic layers, mica fleck and clear quartz depressions like bodies of water seen from the opposite of an aerial view. A cartoon satellite caught me by hook around the neck and kept me from falling fathoms down down down.

Keep going.

Here come the waves.

They roll up from the stomach it seems, something blasting outward from the dantian. I forgot I was a breathing creature until I remembered I had a beating heart. Was I still on the case? The mind was struggling with its own weird landscape. I watched it shine and shudder like a baseball made of fiber-optic strands of light. I was trapped for a moment in wonder. Then something shifted. I thought, I'm getting out of here.

I've had enough experience of experience to remember how to breathe. So, I breathed and the air coming out swirled like a spiral of serpent's breath. What's this music? Some other? And what's that smell? Uh oh, I thought I was starting to fall down the well, and you know what that means, where time works like acid and with stained glass eyes you see time fly…

Radiant stove, radiant black windows glowing back a watery reflection of all this, the pots hanging from the rack like Easter Island heads and the dream catcher with fine dust embedded like pollen on its black strands, the boomerang from Australia with its dreamtime fine-touch pointillist tracks going back in all directions and the oven mitts like slugs caught in flight and jars full of pens and pencils wriggling like worms come up from the flood rains and white paper waiting for a world or a stain and the hard log fibers down there like a forest of infinitesimal terrain and the incredible shrinking man looking up from a sheet of onion skin waving his arms like the castaway he was and the fly the circling fly leaving red trails in its wake and the throbbing liquid floor and walls and so much more and there you are you handsome devil you, like some cave creature with fat hands pawing at the book of mysteries and these unintelligible symbols—man in the maze—and behind the theremin music vibrating his skeletal structure stands the man in the bright nightgown! I turned and closed my eyes and saw the fire of the rose light up. I looked again. He was gone. And in his place the oblivion ah ha shape remained from which he came. I'm getting out of here! But I was going nowhere. Well, I guess I needed a miracle.

"Hey, Angeline!"

Te deum laudamus.

Did I say that or think it? I felt like my head was in a diving bell, heavy and rolling on my shoulders. How did I keep myself up? I felt the entire genetic weight of the dinosaurs.

Movement was fishlike, meaning, I moved but felt like I was swimming, by which I mean I think I was more conscious in the moment of the medium I was in, as if as they say the fish could know it's in water, or something like that. That's the way thoughts were coming, arranging themselves like Chinese silk screens after the fact...the fact, the fact of what? The facts were anything but factual! Zipadee Doo Dah! When did my face take on so much woe?

"I've got to go," I said.
"Then go."
"No, I mean—come with me."
"Oh, I—"
"Just for a walk."
"Oh. Okay."

The brutal clumsy imperfect reach of my actual hand out there, mechanical and adumbrated, cantilevered and flesh-heavy in the garden overhung with thick-shouldered ivy, and Angeline's candle there in the middle on the Celtic design of the iron table, inside its little storm chamber glowing like a soul inside the cell, and flowing in from further out there still came the tribal rhythms of the night along with the swan kiss of a breeze with jasmine floating fluid and sly, and then I am this thinking thought and the words that rise up here and now are what I am now. Then, I think behind the thought. And what I see and feel and understand—not know but understand, and the difference is like trying to command that bell head and that octopus arm and that tongue on fire. How do you control the tongue on fire and the fire that is there and always there just waiting for the right conditions to appear—understand? And you, woman, there before me, launching through the complete evolutionary trajectory in a single breath, you other, you living landlord of the flesh, ah that's it, that's what he meant, but before I could connect it back to the page I had moved ahead, see, yes as primary as a letter, aleph…rising monstrous and divine with me and saying, take my hand…and so out we went into the liquid night.

Let me tell you about wandering and the people appearing and approaching—they were not people at all but their essential selves, spheres glowing blue orange and green and odd fluttering up and down on avenues fringed with mock orange assailing us with sweet profusive scents of orient and memory tails whipping up my thalamic avenues into vivid walks through Berkeley hills with trumpet vines and bear stars coming down like a net floating with a billion eyes looking in and out of galaxies under Carl Sagan's floppy tartan tonsure black matter head, and what a grin Alki has, the grand beast carnival we cut through slow with too much proximity and then down to the beach with the moon as big as a candy skull coming up out of the grave sea with mariachi music and eyes like pinwheels all sapphire and ruby and gold, and great Scott how I was dealing with the warping and wafting of this mechanical tendril marionette body we call I am, struggling to walk as I sent hard intentional electrical bolts like in those old war movies where the captain up on the bridge cranks the brass chadburn to all-ahead-full and then wait and wait and wait for the orders to arrive and take effect and to feel the reaction occur—something like that is how I felt, moving through thick molasses shore air vaguely unsure that I was actually going to be able to pull it off, this whole walking thing, such that I get it, I get you're walking and you don't always realize it but you're also falling and with each step you fall forward slightly and catch yourself from falling and this is how you can be walking and falling at the same time…and the waves come up on the beach and the sand is a soft mattress underfoot and the moon glow is a silent spectral serpent bending through the water...

And then I was alone among the elements. "Hey, where'd you go?" I said.

"I'm right here."

"Where?"

"You can't see the invisible woman?"

"Ha."

Remember, lightning rises from the ground, and so she plied herself from the warm velvet air like a wind-inflated advertisement for mystery vehicles and time-share vacations.

"You having trouble, there, space cowboy?"

"Only with location."

"Then look at your hands."

"Those eye-pilfering ex-convicts?"

"And you call yourself an investigator."

How do you respond to something like that when you're stuck in a worm-hole moment, and the idea of reason is a green snake biting its own tail?

"...out of a paper bag..." I heard, but it might have been me.

What street is this oh mad theater director, what missing person is this on the hand-made notice on the wall? Let's see...unfamiliar face on fluttering sheet, the man missing now since New Year's Eve and last seen at the Alki Tavern which itself is now gone gone gone, and how haven't I heard of this missing person from the collective callosum and where oh where have you gone oh missing dream within the dream among the people orbs floating around, and what philosophy says I am the author of all this?

And the buildings like models of buildings, waffle-shaped apartments and the shake-wall bunker palace and the black spiral stairs we ascend turning turning untethered to lofty perch to gaze from rooftop high and behold like Otto Rank the bombing of London and the fire emerging and glowing and the whole city blazing down to these simple beach fires in their rings glowing morphic in their overlapping, meaning that just is, no reasoning or knowing but we understand. And on we went, down the alleyway and under the palm trees and the hiss-hiss of bamboo tongues and past the back of the log house covered in more wisteria vines and the whicker man's eye in the center of the skeletons dangling in the cedar branches with starfish and sea horses and fluorescent fish netting with little candles flickering over backyard brick garden walls with pit fires glowing and shadows moving around and casting themselves high.

Mermaid on a sign pointing this way to the beach and nautical ropes hanging looped over white fences and more cedar and more sweet-briar—sweet briar!—and a cloaked couple with two kids drifting by with these words coming out of them...

"Many a scrape!"
And the child asks, "What's a maniscape?"
"No, we've had many a scrape..."

This way to the egress.

And the uneven plates of the ground create a tectonic challenge to straight maneuvering.

Battery block townhouses, smell of clams and seashore rocks and seaweed floating its green tendrils through the avenues and through our hair and eyes and mouths, my god don't ask what that sound is, king before the kingdom asking who has caused all this, and a beach chair up there on a hook on the landing is Duchamp's *Nude Descending a Staircase*...

A man rides by on a bicycle with these words coming out of his shirt:

Alive
&
Well

And I saw a satyr moving beside me, a fleshy shadow of my secret mind running and knowing, and that's the house with the gimp in the basement near the surf shop and tattoo parlor, and I caught the scent of cedar smoke again from a backyard fire, and Angeline appeared again in her peregrine wonder wheel lightsphere, and through her I saw the ghost that precedes us and the tracers that follow us and how each time we stop we fall...

"How do you do that?" I said.
"What's that, Lancelot?"
"Two places at once?"
"More than two, buckaroo..."
"What about surveillance cameras?"
"The whole ball of wax is malleable."
"And this was a common activity for you two?"
"He called it edge work."
"Edge work?"
"You have to peer around the edges if you want to see beyond your own reflection."
"Edge work."
"He liked to 'blow off the cobwebs' as he would say."

Up above the nest of Orion and The Bear and Venus one bright singular eye in the heavens looked down as we arrived in the field behind Whale Tale Park, and into that black soupy meadow we went together, little wish luminarias floating like sluggish fireflies in the night among the glow of homes embedded in the hillside, and there I caught the sonic wave that was maybe emanating from propellers on a tanker ship out in the Sound reverberating off of the Alki Community Center walls and back and around in a swirl-current I found my way to the center of and lifted my arms and spinning sent out my own dark waves from the vortex, and I heard the echo of a baseball bat crack shot and music of wind chimes on porches and low rhythmic ancient shifting from deep in the land of a thousand years a thousand more a thousand miles deep...

Past a fence made of wagon wheels we made our way, and entering the intersection we stopped both of us in blind stupid wonder...

"My god..." I said.

58

"What happened?"

"I don't know."

And we both stood there in mute nostril agony staring at the gray crossroad expanse of the street so wide you couldn't go around it telescoping and rolling so that we both saw and felt it in the same pioneer instant, and we laughed like soft mad children at how we never saw it before and how our perfections would always be denied on this road, this road widening like a river in flood swelling, this road no one goes down...

"My god."

"Incredible."

And it seemed impossible to ever cross it.

And the changer changed the land and changed our shapes and changed our way of thinking and seeing and speaking. Who knows what we really said and in what Ur tongue as we strode the grainy gray emulsion of the asphalt through the neighborhood and back to her garden where it all began and where I sat down on the couch, the very same couch, and looked out at the green glowing sea anemones puffing and floating in that grotto chamber dream caesura ante room as I clawed at consciousness around me like a rubbery egg shell and at last at last let go...

Stephen Cooper

Isaac Babel

In the summer of 197-, after a fugitive year overseas—
Åland, Ios, Lamu, Catalina—I found myself back in Los
Angeles. I was broke and nameless and starving for life. My
friend Den Gillis, a working screenwriter, took me in.

Den lived off the Pasadena Arroyo in a house filled
with books. A few years earlier he had had a lucrative run of
feature development deals, none of which survived to the
screen. Lately, to pay for his wife's treatment in a private
sanitarium back east, he'd been churning out tv scripts for a
couple of cop and detective shows.

Den had never been a cop or a detective but now his
days were consumed with plotting out telegenic crimes and
last-minute resolutions. Nights were for drinking, watching
baseball, and talking writers. Den was a serious reader—
about his own writing he held few illusions. Except for me
and my dented Olivetti Lettera, the only other presence in
that house was the memory of Den's wife Finn, short for
Philomene, a revenant force that could lay Den low for days.

Then, sometimes, if I sensed one of his spells coming
on, I would tempt fate double-clutching my way downtown
to loiter along Broadway or Main to the corner of Fifth and
Los Angeles, where you could forget your cares swapping
lies with the other lost souls in that glorious skid-row
hellhole the King Edward Saloon.

But Den had it worse. He had watched Finn lose her
starburst ingénue's mind, and now all he seemed to expect
from life was a back bent double to the whims of the Industry
and an unending spool of misery. Still, he encouraged me.

In June, for example, he persuaded an art director
acquaintance from the American Film Institute to offer me a
job hauling props. The show was non-union, cash in hand
every day, plus the set, this guy promised, would be
swarming with women.

60

I turned him down.

I was hardly twenty-three but already I knew, better go hungry, or to jail, or out on the streets than to settle for less than your own way. Deep down it pleased me to see my father, and his father, and his father before him setting their jaws in approval. Workers, fighters, drinkers, rogues—I meant to extend the line.

Den's head bobbed back and forth as he listened to me rant, his eyes brimming with bliss and dread.

In July my luck took an only-in-L.A. swerve. Den's agent knew an agent who knew a manager who had a client, Sonny Almelah, a bona-fide Movie-of-the-Week mogul. Almelah's stay-at-home wife was said to be dying to make films of her own, not small-screen ephemera but quality theatrical releases—adaptations, no less, of the stories of Isaac Babel. This was a rumor that enflamed me, made my chest ache for the chance. Babel was one of those writers Den had gotten me crazy for—George Borrow, Knut Hamsun, Malcolm Lowry, the Bowleses—and now he was recommending me to help Alana Almelah launch this irresistible dream. He made a phone call. I got the interview.

The next day, sporting one of Den's roomy houndstooths, I took off across town for the Almelahs'. The address was on Cliffside at the tip of Point Dume, a blinding bluff-top pile overlooking the bay. There was a gate and an intercom and a long curving driveway, and when I stepped out of the car at the top of the crest a gust of brine filled my lungs. "Henry Miller," I whispered, "pray for me," and rang the seashell door chime.

A fair-haired Mexican girl in a fitted smock ushered me in. Everywhere I looked glass walls glimmered behind bright frameless canvases that seemed to float in mid-air. The *rubia* too seemed to float as she walked, and with that eye of hers—it was lazy, that was the thing—I thought she must like looking back when she screwed.

She left me in the living room to ponder my sins for a minute before another woman glided in. This one's hair shined dark like her eyes and the way she moved was a study. And why not? Alana Almelah was one of those wives, no longer thirty, poised between the firmness of youth and surrender to a softer age. Since bible times, her walk seemed to say, such women have satisfied husbands who take pleasure in showing off their worth in so much ripe supple olive-green flesh.

She pressed my hands between jeweled fingers, and I swear to God said, "Isaac Babel is my greatest love!"

The story she planned to start with was "Guy de Maupassant." In fact, she had already begun a treatment, there it was right in front of me, typed pages strewn across a buttery divan.

She hovered while I skimmed. My aim was to discover if the manuscript held anything for me—nor was I disappointed. Babel's style, as sharp as whetted steel, had been dulled to crumpled tinfoil. Here was a woman who wrote like a schoolgirl practicing her penmanship. I pictured her biting her tongue, squinting to stay inside the lines, a member of that vast legion of readers with taste but no talent.

I folded the pages, promised to return the next day, and barreled back to Pasadena.

"Roll over, Billy Wilder!" Den said when I showed him the job. "Now get upstairs and hit it."

Dawn was seeping through the curtains by the time I finished breathing life into Alana's efforts. The work wasn't as bad as it might seem. When a story is born, as Babel tells us, it is both good and bad—the way to success is barely discernible: *One's fingertips must grasp the key, gently warming it. And then the key must be turned once, not twice.*

I turned the key and fell asleep, soaring.

Later that day I returned with my revisions. Alana's belief in Babel's potential for cinematic greatness was coming true, she was certain. As I read aloud what I had written she sat forward rubbing her shoulders, mouthing phrases. A mottled flush rose upon her throat.

"Where did you learn to do this?"

I told her about how writers read, about living inside the story like a sniper, or a spy, until you have transformed its secrets into your own. My hands were cold. An icy finger on her heart might have driven home the point but she kept me reading, it was clear, to prolong the moment. Her lips were glossy, parted, trembling, her hair caught sparks of light, and her legs, singing arias of the deepest belief, kept crossing higher and higher.

La rubia, looking away, appeared with our lunch.

The sovereign sunlight of Los Angeles streamed in through the window, warming the carpet, the sofa, my knees. On the table before us lay Babel's *You Must Know Everything*. One ray crept over the rough-cut edges of the volume—a sleeping volcano of human savagery and desire.

We sipped lemon water from cut crystal and set to work. "My First Fee" came next, Babel's turn on the classic boy-to-man tale, though the lusty Vera of the pointed nipples ends by calling our hero "little sister." Little sister—ha! For the shameless love-struck writer-to-be learns the seductive cunning of story, mesmerizing the wench with words stolen from novels until *she* pays *him* for his innocence.

I returned to Pasadena with Alana's down payment, a personal check of one thousand dollars. That night Den and I knocked off half a bottle of rum, chasing it with cold beer after beer. I barbecued a sagging pair of rib eyes, exhorting Den to clean his plate, then fell to railing against the disastrous theory of the auteur.

"Orson Welles? That mountebank? If it hadn't been for—for—"

"Herman J. Mankiewicz," Den said.

"—if it hadn't been for Herman J. Mankiewicz, the old fat man would still be doing parlor tricks for a living instead of flogging rotgut wine."

The meat was doing its work. Color was returning to Den's cheeks, though you could still see the darting in his eyes.

"Don't move," he said and lurched up the stairs.

When he came back down he was clutching a pillow to his Pendleton. I thought he was going to curl up and crash but no, he pulled off the slip to thrust the ticking in my face. I backed away but he kept pressing, making sure I saw the scabby encrustations and smelled the fetid stale-spit stench.

"Get it?" Den said. "You see what I'm saying? She'd start and she couldn't stop, all day and all night. Scratching, till everything was blood."

I passed out on the couch into a brutal dream. Before Finn had suffered her breakdown I had hardly known her, and then only in a young-writer-coming-to-visit-older-writer kind of way, with Finn the demure wife making herself small in the background. Since moving into the house I had seen her likeness only once, when I turned over one of the framed photos that Den now kept face-down in every room. But for the rest of that night in a dream that kept repeating Finn and I devoured each other like cannibals.

In the morning I drifted into the kitchen, head pounding. Den was already at the table, bent over the National League box scores. He sat nursing a 16-ounce can of Lite, just another fan whose bride had earned an Oscar nomination for her debut film performance then plunged into irreversible despair.

Den looked up, his face a ruin, and forced a smile.

"My Cubbies," he said. "God love 'em all the way to the grave."

After that I took my breakfasts at the Almelahs', huevos rancheros, pan dulce, and enough strong Mexican coffee to power me through the day's work. By then I'd had the clutch in my car repaired but at the end of any shift Alana might insist we cool down by taking her canary-yellow 450-

SL convertible up the coast. I would steer us past Zuma and Trancas and the Navy's missile warfare station at Point Mugu and she would ask me to tell her about how I had grown up. I didn't want to do that but she persisted. The story that emerged was strange and mournful. My eyes on the road, I felt the grip of her attention like the aura before a migraine, and below the highway the pitiless rolling of the swells.

Eventually Alana introduced me to her husband, a bullet-headed manic who worked out in his office-gym and was forever flexing, even in his cufflinks. People whispered about his family ties to the Shah of Iran, maybe even SAVAK. The man's fortune—founded on his invention of the world's first quick-stop lube-and-oil franchise and parlayed into an empire of television melodrama—had left him with an expression of permanent giddiness. Only later did I realize how badly he embarrassed Alana.

Near the end of summer Alana's sisters—she was the middle of three—drove up with their husbands from Newport and La Jolla, respectively. The visit cost us a whole week of work. We had broken off in the middle of "The Kiss" but I kept at it on my own, and when I was finished I brought the script over early one evening. The lazy eye of the blond maid said to wait while she announced me. From another room came brassy laughter, the men's in bursts, the women's tinkling. Alana appeared in something shimmery and strapless, wobbling on ankle-ribbon espadrilles, chunky bracelets flashing silver and gold.

"Why there you are, you, you—"

She raised an imaginary glass, hitched her shoulders and fanned her hair, then did a little sideways step before collapsing upon a pharaonic settee. Beneath the shadow of her collarbone pulsed a vein.

More bursting, tinkling laughter gave way to her husband's entrance with the others, all primed for a night on the town. Like Alana, both her sisters ferried their breasts before them, pampered women of a perilous age born to

65

carry on the banter while their husbands patted pockets for matches and keys. They were almost out the door, on their way to the Palm and a private screening, when Alana suffered a sudden change of heart.

"I want my work to live!" she cried and sent the others on without her, the five protesting to no avail. One more group laugh to convince themselves, and they were gone.

A moment later she had me uncorking a dusty bottle and filling two chiseled goblets.

"Clos du Val '72," she said. "Worth dying for if Sonny discovers us."

But the discovery was mine, first one glass then another. The toasts to life sailed back and forth like battlefield volleys even as a flickering alcove drew us in.

"So, now, where did we leave off?" Alana asked.

"'The Kiss'?" It wasn't a question.

"I love it when you remind me where we are."

It was August in Babel's story, and the war was veering around. The Poles have taken the town of Budziatycze but the Red Cavalry have won it back, raking the line with machine gun fire from careening *tachankas*. Billeted in the home of the village schoolmaster, war correspondent Kiril Vasilyevich Lyutov finds himself enchanted by the old man's daughter.

"She's up for it," Lyutov's orderly muses. "She just hasn't come out and said it."

And yet, her housedress clinging, Elizaveta Alekseyevna looks at Lyutov with eyes made bright by the hope that he will take her away to another life in Moscow.

One flaming evening Lyutov's orderly drives them in a wicker horse cart up the hill to an abandoned castle. Amidst the rubble Lyutov pulls Elizaveta Alekseyevna toward him. Uncertain and confused, she flees. Later that night he slips into her room to find her reading.

"No," she says, staring up at him, "please, dearest, no." And embracing his head with her long bare arms she gives him a violent, silent kiss—a silence shattered by the piercing trumpet call to arms. The brigade is ordered to outflank the Poles, who have broken through again. Galloping away, Lyutov turns to see Elizaveta Alekseyevna in her batiste nightdress, lamplight bathing her nape.

I refilled our glasses and again—"To life."

"To life!"

The maid passed through the room taking her leave.

After riding without rest for a hundred kilometers, Lyutov joins the fight, which turns into a rout, and then an endless muddy retreat. Lyutov dozes in his saddle through a late summer downpour, losing all sense of time and direction. One night, quartered in a country church, he realizes he is only a nine-verst ride from Budziatycze. To leave would be desertion—his horse is a staggering ribcage—and yet off he rides. He finds Elizaveta Alekseyevna in the same sheer nightdress, and they steal off into a shed stacked with winter potatoes and beehive frames to discover where the path from the ruined castle was always leading…

Alana exhaled. She raised her glass.

"To Babel!"

"To the castle path!"

I inhaled the peppery sweetness of her breath.

"You devil you," she murmured, falling back against the wall. Her arms made a cross—all that was missing were the nails. "You're a funny one alright."

I drained my glass. A summer night, a vintage bottle, and the shattering power of Babel's lines had so conspired that I flung the book open and declaimed:

"During the 'Social Revolution' nobody has had finer intentions than the People's Commissariat of Welfare. Its schemes are audacious indeed. It has been entrusted with tasks of the highest importance: to produce an immediate explosion in the soul of man, to usher in by decree a reign of universal love, and to prepare citizens for a life of dignity in free communes."

"Comrade," Alana snarled, "we have our orders."

Before the others had returned, I was gone from that bloated palace. Down the Coast Highway then over the freeways I veered from lane to lane, belting out an anthem that seemed to invent itself as I drove.

Den was asleep on the couch when I came in, sports section splayed over his chest. Even unconscious his face looked pained, as if he were seeing the ghost of his beloved Finn; but waking him would only hurt more. I slipped up to my room, switched on the reading light, and opened Conquest's indispensable meditation on the Great Terror.

That night I began to learn some facts.

After dazzling revolutionary Russia with his early stories Babel had joined the Red Army's doomed invasion of Poland. His fellow troops were Jew-hating Cossacks so he adopted a Russian-sounding name in order to write what he was witnessing—men shot to meat, castrated, stomped to death—women gang raped and cut open—children starving for milk. As Stalin's madness spiraled, Babel published less and less, but even a retreat into state-sanctioned screenwriting failed to quench his need to know. Despite the known risks he continued visiting a certain woman, wife of the head of the NKVD, in the hope of discovering "a key to the puzzle"—until one night he was arrested, imprisoned, tortured, and shot, his body disposed of, his writings made to vanish with his name...

I closed the book and moved barefoot to the window. Veils of mist rose from the Arroyo like souls ascending. I thought of my father, how he had died, and myself, just starting out, shivering, full of piss, almost immortal.

Emily Elbom

Good Work, Sister
(1944)

Union Station was busy—men in uniform, porters, women with kids. Max squinted in the bright Los Angeles sunshine. The trains, the noise, the long rows of posters: LONGING WON'T BRING HIM HOME, GET A WAR JOB! MY GIRL'S A WOW! KEEP 'EM SMILING WITH LETTERS FROM FOLKS AND FRIENDS—WRITE AND WRITE OFTEN. He shaded his eyes with his hands. The poster closest to him showed a picture of a shiny roadster, driven by a happy couple. The picture was crossed out with a large red X. It said: IS YOUR TRIP NECESSARY? NEEDLESS TRAVEL INTERFERES WITH THE WAR EFFORT. However, the couple certainly looked like they were having fun. He wished he had a car, that'd he'd driven, that if it had to be the train he could have at least had a whole Pullman to himself. But even if he had a car, he reminded himself, he probably wouldn't have had the gas—not these days, anyway. He put his suitcase under his arm and got in the first empty taxi.

A female voice: Where to?

Max rubbed the sun out of his eyes. A woman rested one hand on the steering wheel, draped the other around the front seat.

Surprised, are you, the woman said.

No, not really, Max said. I suppose you drive for the war. Nothing surprising in that.

He thought she looked like of one of the poster girls, the pretty redhead, with her fingers pressed to red lips: SILENCE MEANS SECURITY.

This woman didn't have red lips, but the red hair was styled the same way. She had both hands on the wheel now, and her head was tilted just so, but he didn't say where he wanted to go—although he did have places he must go,

69

errands to attend to, limited time. But really, he thought, what's the rush.

She fiddled with the meter and asked him again where he wanted to go.

Oh, I don't know, why don't you take me around, show me Los Angeles, beaches, all those picture stars they say are supposed to be frolicking about.

I'll tell you what, she said. She was looking at him through the rearview mirror. You're my last fare of the afternoon. I'll take the long way back to the garage, and no one will know I wasted gas. If you see something interesting, just tell me to stop.

He said OK. She started driving. At the red light she stopped next to a black Mercedes driven by a woman wearing a leopard print hat and dark glasses. Max leaned out the window. The car was clearly from the thirties, well taken care of, as was the woman. Visible in the windshield was a letter A—civilian gas, four gallons a week. The woman in the dark glasses didn't look at him. He turned back to the taxi driver, who was still staring at him in the rearview mirror.

I wouldn't be caught driving that if I was her, she said.

Max shrugged. It's a good car, even if it is a bit older, he said.

She looked at him some more. He knew his answer wasn't the right one. FUEL FOR THEM MEANS LESS FOR YOU. She smiled anyway. The light changed; the taxi jolted forward.

My name's Corrine.

She smiled and kept driving, kept asking questions, kept looking at him in the damned mirror. What's your name? Are you a soldier? Why aren't you overseas? Navy mortuary personal? An assistant? In San Francisco? Are you on leave? Have you been here before? Do you like my new dress? Am I asking too many questions?

Max answered politely—she wasn't bad-looking. Nosey, maybe, but he liked her voice. She told him there was only a block to go. He told her to stop, to let him off at the drugstore on the corner, to drive the taxi back to the garage and come back and meet him. She agreed, and as soon as she agreed he felt a little sick. He shifted the suitcase across his knees. He knew he should have taken care of the letter first, like he'd promised, before picking up taxi girls, before enjoying the sun, or whatever he was supposed to enjoy here.

At the lunch counter in the drugstore Max waited — first ten minutes — then fifteen. He drank a cup of coffee. He checked his watch. He walked over and looked at the motion picture magazines, *Photoplay* and then *Movie Land*. He'd started drinking a cherry coke when she came in and sat down next to him. She apologized: had to park, the boss, that kind of thing. Max asked what she wanted, told her it was on him.

They sat there, side by side, waiting for their fried eggs and toast. Max asked a few polite questions, where was she from, if she had sisters, how'd she become a taxi driver, of all things, even in the middle of a war. She giggled and said she'd started as a welder. She'd left school at seventeen, which, she said, seemed like the patriot thing to do. It was those posters. Her mother disapproved, even if it was patriotic. Mothers always do, Max said. He put his hand on her arm. The eggs and toast came. She told him she lied about her age and got hired by a shipfitter, took a two-week course, and became a tacker. After a few months she was promoted to a journeyman welder. She liked welding, maybe even better than driving a taxi, but the arc, the flash burns, hurt her eyes. You didn't really think about it at the time, but she'd be out with friends and her eyes would start tingling, the sting would increase, and then for a few hours she wouldn't be able to see a single thing.

Max nodded. He was sitting very close to her, he knew she was watching him, but he was afraid to look at her. She was playing with her eggs, pushing them up onto the toast.

Once, she said, she'd been out with a sailor and it happened. Only he didn't believe her. He thought she was trying to get out of the date. He yelled at her, told her she was shirking her civic duties, a night on the town to get him

71

through years at sea, that kind of nonsense. Thought she didn't like him, just walked off and left her, alone, and blind. She didn't even know exactly where she was. Besides, she hadn't liked him.

Max shook his head and told her she shouldn't date sailors. He should know. He'd done enough shore patrols.

But you're in the Navy, she said. Maybe I shouldn't be out with you.

I'm not a sailor.

You're worse, she said, laughing. You touch dead ones.

She put her hand on top of Max's hand, the hand that was still on her arm. Her fingernails were carefully rounded, and she had nice white moons.

That doesn't explain why you're driving a taxi now, he said.

But it does, she said. When that sailor left her, blind, she started crying right there on the sidewalk. She thought maybe the tears would help. After a few minutes a taxi driver pulled over and took her home. Her mother answered the door and, hearing what had happened, wouldn't let her weld anymore, or date sailors.

Naturally, Max said.

Her mother thanked the taxi driver and insisted that he stay for coffee. He said that he actually owned the taxi company, and was looking for capable girls, that most of his men had left and joined the war. That is, if her eyes went back to normal and she could pass a vision test. The next day she quit welding and took up driving.

She went quiet. Max sneaked a look at her eyes. They were green and didn't show any signs of damage.

But what if your eyes had never gone back to normal, what if you'd stayed blind?

Then he said I could be a radio girl—a taxi dispatcher.

They looked at each other and laughed. The old man behind the counter came back with a single slice of pie. On the house, he said. He winked at Max. Corrine took her hand off of Max's but she didn't move her arm out from under his hand. Max didn't know what to do. He looked at the old man. He looked at the pie and his toast and eggs. He thought about the woman with the hat and the dark glasses. He looked down at the suitcase and thought about the letter. He wondered where Corrine's sailor was now. Maybe in the Pacific. Dead, maybe, with his dog tags kicked into his teeth. Corrine was watching him again, he could tell. He turned his head and looked at the fan magazines.

Have you ever met any picture stars?

You run into them now and then, Corrine said.

Really?

Once I saw Groucho Marx eating a cheese sandwich at a lunch counter down on Sunset.

Did he have his cigar?

No. My friend Nina works at Paramount as a typist and gets invited to parties occasionally. She's always allowed to bring a date, and on occasion, she brings me.

But you're a girl.

Since when has anyone complained about an extra single girl at a party?

Sure, sure.

Well, it's not exactly the real reason, Corrine said. You can bring a girl on account of the lack of eligible bachelors in America these days.

Max nodded. He looked down at his suitcase. His hand started to sweat on her arm. He doubted Corrine noticed, or cared. She seemed happy to talk. Maybe it was a skill she picked up as a cab driver. LOOSE LIPS SINK SHIPS. He started thinking about the telegrams, how they mostly read the same. The Secretary of War deeply regrets to inform you that your (husband, son, brother) (name) was killed in action in (the Pacific, Europe, Germany, whatever area) (date) while (action). The Navy (or Army, or whatever branch) expresses profound sympathy, etc. Confirming letter follows.

The Navy never actually delivered the telegrams. That was a job for Western Union. But just the same, everyone in the Navy knew what they said. Once, wandering in San Francisco on a day off, he'd watched a Western Union boy, about sixteen, approach a house. The boy had walked quickly—in retrospect, Max thought, to avoid the neighbors. A very old man across the street had stopped sweeping the sidewalk, leaned for a moment on the broom, dropped it, and ran up the steps into his house. Max stopped walking and watched the boy ring the doorbell. A woman wearing curlers answered the door. She took the telegram. The boy said he was sorry. The woman opened her mouth, surprised, and then slammed the door. Max stood still. The Western Union boy stood still. The old man who'd been sweeping came back out of his front door, along with a very old woman, and they both ran and knocked on the woman's door. The Western Union boy turned around, stuck his hands in his pockets, and walked away down the street. And Max, you old son of a bitch, he thought, you just kept standing there.

He looked at Corrine. She was still talking.

Well, if I can get an invite for tonight, would you come with me or not?

Yes, Max said. He wasn't sure what else to say.

Hold on, I'll call my friend at Paramount. Got a dime?

She was gone a while. Max put money down on the counter. The old man came back and took the plates, even the pie, which was untouched. He didn't say anything, but he was still smiling. Corrine came back and Max half rose out of his seat. She shook her head. Nothing doing. Not tonight, anyway. But tomorrow night, if Max was still willing, her friend could give them invitations to a rather exclusive party, one that benefited the Hollywood Canteen. If he could wear his uniform, look official, he wouldn't have to dress up. That is, she said, if you don't have other plans, other people to see.

When he didn't say anything she said that she could pick him up on her last taxi run, and then they could take the bus to her friend's apartment. Her friend had a car, gas even, she'd drive them to the party along with her date. Max stood and picked up his suitcase. He told her it all sounded good. Except for one thing, something he had to get done tomorrow. He'd promised, he said.

What is it?

I have to deliver a letter to a girl.

Corrine frowned.

She isn't my girl, Max said. She's a relative of the head pathologist. Maybe a niece, or a cousin twice removed, I can't exactly remember. Her husband was killed.

Corrine's mouth opened slightly.

She knows he's dead, he said. She's already gotten the telegram. But they always send a confirming letter, usually by mail. This is just a favor, a personal favor. He patted the suitcase—the letter's in here.

Corrine smiled, and said: Well, how about I pick you up and take you in my taxi. You'll have to get there somehow. You can be my last fare.

Sure, Max said. Sure.

He slept badly that night. He didn't dream. He woke up sweating. He put slippers on, went down to the hotel desk and asked for a postage stamp.

At this hour?

Please, it's important.

The desk clerk rummaged around behind the desk and shook his head. Can't it wait until morning?

In the morning he hung his uniform in the bathroom, hoping that a hot shower would steam out some of the wrinkles. He wanted to do this neatly, have the whole day go neatly. He showered and shaved neatly. He left his uniform hanging, put on yesterday's street clothes and went down the block to eat breakfast. The sun was bright, and he wished for

75

sunglasses. He read the paper, folded it up neatly, walked up and down the block, paced his room, bought a hotdog for lunch, sent a telegram home, then a postcard (*Greetings from Hollywood*). An hour later he bought a new pair of socks, went back to his room, took another shower, and sat naked in front of the desk fan, waiting.

It wasn't that he didn't know what to say, or what to do, and the letter, after all, wasn't unexpected. No, something else bothered him. He looked at his new socks, then at his old ones. They were still perfectly good, just dirty. He never wanted to wear them again. USE IT UP, WEAR IT OUT, AND MAKE DO. He sat on the bed and thought about the beginning. The fog, the hills, the coast. The Navy pathologist, an older man, had told Max that normally he'd have been considered too old for service, but his long career as a medical examiner in the Bay Area made service possible, required even. If no one else is around, he said, Max could just call him Bill. Bill showed him the ropes. He showed him how to get the body on the table, how to record the weight of organs, label little vials of blood, how to line cotton wool into the cavity and sew it shut, how to disinfect the table and his hands. It was only after he was done, that first day, that Max asked about the man that they'd taken apart, put back together, and wrapped up. Who was he? Where'd he come from? Bill looked at the charts he was carrying. Accident at the docks, possible intoxication, never even made it to the Pacific, not even out to sea. Bill shook his head and watched Max. Normally, Bill said, we're not this thorough—they don't often send us overseas casualties anymore, just bury them where they fall, and the few that die here we look over and send home. As an afterthought he said, in the last war, I was a medic.

Later, after another shower, Max put on his uniform and new socks. He rolled his old socks up and hid them under the mattress. He was late, and when the desk clerk from the night before asked if he'd found a stamp, he didn't answer. Corrine was waiting for him, leaning against the passenger door, her hair covered with a kerchief, her hands in her jean pockets.

She patted her head. I got it done. After you've played mailman we'll stop at my place so I can change, and then we'll return the taxi and wait for our ride to the party. We won't even have to take the bus.

Max nodded. She opened the passenger door and told him that on this trip she'd feel better if he sat up front. As she drove he kept glancing at her. She stared straight ahead — except once he caught her looking at the typed address on the envelope sitting on his lap. IF YOU TELL WHERE HE'S GOING, HE MAY NEVER GET THERE. She drove for a very long time, past palm trees and parked cars, bars and beaches, hotels and hospitals. She parked in front of a little yellow bungalow. The paint was peeling. A baby buggy sat in the yard. The house next door looked the same, except it was painted white.

Technically, we're not in Los Angeles anymore, Corrine said.

Wait here, Max said.

The woman that answered the door didn't say anything. She took one look at his uniform, at the letter in his hand, and pointed to a sitting room down the hall. Max sat down and she shut the door. She said she knew why he was there. She'd been expecting him, not exactly today, but in general. Max felt bad. She kept touching her hair, nervously. She preferred if they did this quickly, that considering the circumstances, it would be easier on her this way. She said she had told her Uncle Bill that it would have been easier on her if he'd not have intervened — if the letter had just arrived by post. Max thought she looked very small, but very brave. She took a cigarette from a box on the little table next to her chair. Max got up and lit it for her. She took a drag and puffed smoke at him. But you know my Uncle Bill, she said. Always does the right thing. Always thorough.

Not knowing what else to do, and still holding onto the letter, Max started repeating what Bill had told him to say — the words sounded empty now, he wished the woman would cry, or at least look at him. Instead, she puffed smoke at the walls, the room growing hazy. He told her all the little details, that as next of kin she had the right to request what he had been carrying, that he'd been buried overseas, the Graves Registration knew exactly where. He pulled out the letter, waving away the smoke, when from somewhere in the house a baby started crying. The woman snuffed the cigarette and took the envelope.

Is that everything?

Max nodded. I'm truly sorry, I didn't know your husband left a child.

She looked at him, but Max looked away. He hated Bill. DON'T BE A SUCKER, KEEP YOUR MOUTH SHUT.

You don't mind if I don't walk you to the door. The baby, she said.

As Max stood up to leave, a man opened the door. Celia, the man said, the baby's crying.

She looked at the man, and then at Max.
My cousin, she said.
How old is the baby? Max said.
He's quite new, the woman said.
Max looked at the man, who was scowling. Was the woman blushing?

I'll show myself out, Max said.

When he got back to the taxi, Corrine was humming. She'd left the car running. Max got in and told her that he needed to send a telegram right away.

But the party, she said.
Please, he said. It's important.

Max told the kid at Western Union that he wanted a night telegram. Delivered letter to niece and her cousin. Congratulations on your new grandnephew.

It's nice to see a fellow send good news for once, the kid said.

Corrine was waiting, staring at him, as usual.

You didn't have to delay your plans, he said.
I thought you wanted to go to the party, she said.
Two days ago I didn't even know you.

He looked at her green eyes, the tears in the corners. He apologized—told her he wasn't sure what put him in such a bad mood. She should dry her tears. She had such lovely eyes. When she wasn't crying, that is. Him? It was just that damned letter business. Yes, he was sure the party would cheer him up. Yes, she looked alright, even in slacks. Did she know that he always said yes.

At the party everyone laughed and drank, even Max. The drinks were carried around on little silver trays by women who all looked like the woman in the Mercedes. The women wore little red, white, and blue romper suits. There were sailors and soldiers, airmen and army personnel. There were girls, lots of girls, girls from the pictures, from the makeup departments, wardrobe, secretaries—armies of girls. There were stars, well dressed, elegant, wearing ruby, sapphire, and diamond pins, or fine silk bowties. Max recognized their faces, some from when he was very small, some from the magazines, some from the picture shows he'd seen lately. They laughed, and frequently stopped to talk to men in uniforms. Photographers snapped press photos. A newsreel crew sat drinking gin-and-tonics in an out-of-the-way corner. The war effort at home. Corrine couldn't quit pointing. Yes, Max said, yes, I see. Corrine was dressed up. She had on a long yellow evening gown. She wore long gloves—just like Rita Hayworth's. See, we're even wearing the same color. She's across the room, on the other side of the dance floor.

Yes, Max said.

Rita Hayworth's gloves suited her arms so perfectly, and they were gold, not yellow. Corrine's gloves looked too tight, borrowed. He took another drink from a passing silver tray. He missed her blue jeans; he missed the way she draped her arm across the seat of her taxi.

Let's go for a walk, he said, or to a picture show. Or come to San Francisco with me.

She laughed, putting one gloved hand over her mouth.

Please, he said.

The band stopped playing and a girl jumped out of a big white cake. The crowd laughed. Corrine stared. Max's uniform itched. He thought about Bill's niece. It wasn't Bill's fault, Bill obviously didn't know. He couldn't blame her, not really. He looked at Corrine and imagined standing on a ship, her on the shore, waving, they'd worry about life together later, if he came home. And why should she wait? Better not to. AMERICA'S WOMEN HAVE MET THE TEST. The band started again. She held out her hands to dance. Just a minute, he said as he took another glass from the silver tray.

Later: Corrine left the party. Someone, a producer, or director, had seen her from across the room, liked her yellow gloves, and invited her to finish the celebration with a few other guests at his house. Corrine had pointed at Max and asked if he could come too. The man had punched him on the shoulder and said sure, Navy, of course. But Max said no. He didn't feel well. It's the alcohol, Corrine said. The producer, or director, or whoever he was, looked at Max and said that he'd be over in the corner if they decided to join him. He gave a slight bow to Corrine and turned around. Max shrugged and reminded her that he was leaving tomorrow. He was tired, his uniform was dirty, he should really take her home. Or she should really take him home. He looked at her green eyes. One of them, he was sure, was actually hazel, not green at all. She rubbed her nose with her gloves. Her friend, the one who had gotten them the party invites, walked up. Corrine turned and said something in her ear. Max watched the producer talk to the saxophone player from the band. The girl who had jumped out of the cake was now standing next to him.

We're going to that party, Corrine said.

What about going home with me? Max said.

Do you mean it?

He looked at her. He would never leave on a ship, but it could still be nice. He pictured her driving a taxi through the hills of San Francisco. The fog, the sea, the waves. He thought about Bill's niece, the way she filled the room with smoke. He remembered the smell of disinfectant, rows of stainless steel tables. A CARELESS WORD, A NEEDLESS SINKING.

No, he said.

You're just another sailor, she said.

It was late now. Max leaned against the wall in the men's room. The bathroom attendant wiped water off the counter and watched him in the mirror. Max felt sick. He wondered what would happen if he didn't take the train back to the Navy, if they'd send a telegram to his family, or just a couple of men wearing official uniforms. He wondered if Corrine would be the next Rita Hayworth. He felt guilty and decided it must be the new socks. After a while the bathroom attendant asked if he could call him a taxi, or perhaps find one of his friends. Max told him he'd walk. Sir, the bathroom attendant said, no one walks in Los Angeles. So Max took a taxi, and the taxi driver's name was Ned, and Ned didn't say a word. Max paid him and walked into the hotel.

You have a telegram, the desk clerk said.
Can't it wait until morning?
There was a call too, the desk clerk said.
A woman?
A man. San Francisco.

Max took the telegram up to his room. He'd left the bathroom light on, and the fan was still spinning. He hoped the telegram was from Corrine, but he was sure it was from Bill.

It was short. Port Chicago Explosion. Take first morning train. Over 300 dead.

Max put the telegram down on the table, but the blowing fan fluttered it to the floor. He set the alarm clock.

81

He washed his face and brushed his teeth. He hung up his uniform and packed his suitcase. He took off and folded the new socks, and retrieved the old ones from under the mattress, and sat down at the desk. He decided that in the morning he wouldn't get a newspaper to read on the train. The long line of men on the steel tables would tell him everything he needed to know. MATERIALS WASTED MEAN LIVES WASTED. Through the hotel room window he waited for a yellow taxi to drive slowly by.

Gilad Elbom

Battle Lore

In an attempt to enlarge, if only temporarily, her cadre of supervised specialists, my commanding officer had arranged for a junior data encryption officer to be attached to our unit. She came from the division, and her job was to assist us with information security. She worked hard and interacted mostly with the other officers, although it was important for her to communicate to me that showing a certain amount of genuine interest in a simple corporal was not beneath her. She wanted to know what I thought about things, and she wanted me to be honest. She asked if I admired my commanding officer as much as she did. She said that my commanding officer was a true inspiration, and what a privilege it was to work with such a remarkable woman. She could tell that my commanding officer was destined to greatness, and she only wished she could emulate her more wholly, channel some of her energy, learn from her more accurately, etc. She said that she would love to hear, if I didn't mind, about my own contribution to the success of the unit. Maybe over coffee, she said, preferably somewhere outside the base. In fact, she was planning a trip to the north this weekend, and did I want to join her? No pressure, she said. Just a brief excursion. And only if I was interested. I told her I was interested, and she said that she would pick me up on Saturday. Early in the morning, if I had no objection.

At home, I sat with my notebook and tried to describe her. I wanted to capture her essence with one swift sentence but failed, again and again, to find the right words. All I could do was copy sentences from other books. She had a big mouth, and when she laughed, she belatedly caught her lower lip in her teeth, as though she were ashamed of so large a mouth, and her breasts shook. James Baldwin. She had thick eyelashes and the strong shoulders, neck, and thighs of a woman who does heavy work, but her thin nose, her lively and ironic eyes, and her slender ankles meant that she was by no means ordinary in appearance. Ignazio Silone. Her cheekbones were prominent and her forehead high. Her lips were full and half-open as though they had broken away only a moment before from a long, passionate kiss and were not yet sated. Sadeq Hedayat.

She showed up in a beautiful sports car. A present from her father, she said, and shook her head in mock disapproval. It wasn't the latest model, but she liked it. She didn't feel uncomfortable driving such an extravagant vehicle, not at all, although she did find herself, on occasion, obliged to distance herself from some of her expensive possessions, usually by telling her friends, or anyone who cared to listen, that her parents, bless their souls, had always had a bad habit of spoiling her too much. She said that she was hungry, and asked if I was in the mood for a hamburger. She knew the perfect place. A little out of our way, she said, but worth it. I told her I had no objection.

It was, I had to admit, a nice restaurant. She ordered a hamburger with fire-roasted tomatoes, a side salad, and a cup of coffee. I ordered the same. She said that the fact that I hadn't shaved this morning was quite endearing but totally unnecessary. In case I didn't know, there was no need to go, especially not for her sake, through the proverbial trouble of looking excessively masculine. I told her that I had been, in the past, observant, and although I was desecrating the Sabbath, some old practices were hard to forsake. She said she really hated, and this was just her personal outlook, all those religious parasites who sucked the blood of hardworking citizens. To each his own was a valuable platitude, but honestly, she couldn't understand what possessed people in this day and age to put those funny leather straps on their heads and arms, and mumble ancient prayers to an invisible deity, and preach to others about good behavior and bad behavior. When I confessed that I had gone to synagogue twice a day, every day, for many years, she said that she was glad that I had found the wisdom to abandon such superstitions.

84

But wasn't the hamburger delicious? The real McCoy, the genuine article, the big shebang, the whole enchilada, the cat's pajamas, the bee's knees. The kind of hamburger that hit the spot, knocked your socks off, blew you away, tickled you pink, bowled you over, boggled your mind, shivered your timbers, and put hair on your chest. She didn't understand, however, why it was so impossible to serve a decent salad. Not that it mattered, but really, how hard was it for what she assumed was a credentialed cook to learn how to slice a few miserable vegetables? And did they really think we would be happy with such tepid coffee? How much longer would it be before people learned to boil some water in this country? Would she ever live to see the day?

But anyway, it was time to hit the road. Our first destination was Yodfat, also known as Jotapata, where Flavius Josephus had surrendered to Vespasian. She said that our day trip, though seemingly short, was part of a very long journey.

Later that night, at home, I felt ashamed of having portrayed her in such a ridiculous way. I felt compelled to replace her with a new and improved version. Her eyes were splendid, wide, fearless, as free from suspicion as a child's who has never been rebuked. Charlotte Perkins Gilman. She had a Modigliani figure, long-limbed and high-breasted, and was dressed usually in black. Alison Lurie. Her frame was sinewy and slender, as she constantly pursued her daily bread. But her backbone was solid. Her facial features were sharpened by excessive thinness, etched in bone as enduring as stone. Nawal El Saadawi.

In my imagination, she loved to hike but said that to worship the land was to worship real estate. She said that you could be a Hebrew in the north of Israel, in the center of London, or anywhere else in the world, and that her definition of identity was textual, not geopolitical. The ultimate meaning of being Jewish was to study biblical literature, rabbinical literature, and other Jewish texts, and the best place to do that was at home.

Our next destination was Gamla, another site of historical significance, national heroism, and mass suicide, then the River Jordan, where she removed her clothes and jumped in the water. It wasn't a hot day, but she said she felt alive, excited, invigorated. I stood and watched as she alternated between a perfect breaststroke and underwater dolphin kicks, both equally graceful. It was a marvelous show, and her intentions were clear. She climbed out of the water and squeezed her hair. She had two towels in the car, one of which she wrapped around her body, the other she spread on the ground. We sat in the sun. She asked if I wasn't frustrated being a simple soldier. She could tell I had potential; she could tell I could excel, and she wanted me to know, just in case I was thinking about the future, that it wasn't too late for officer school. It was certainly the best decision she had made in her life.

I told her that my goal was to remain unnoticed, and she said she hoped I was joking. She could really see me, if I didn't mind her saying so, enjoying the benefits, not to mention the inner rewards—the sheer satisfaction—that came with responsibility. She said she would be happy to share her thoughts about me, which were mostly positive, with my commanding officer. She truly believed that if I managed to suppress my innate misanthropy, or tone it down a little, the sky would be the limit. Of course, I wouldn't be able to squander my life on reading and writing, but I could always, in my spare time, watch movies. Unless, she said, I thought that movies were a waste of time.

In my mind, we talked about speculative cinema. We disagreed, but I was patient and attentive, never dismissive of her opinions or observations. In my mind, we discussed an experimental film set in a future universe marked by peace and harmony. Weapons hadn't been in existence for centuries, and war was considered a primitive manifestation of insecurity, neurotic recklessness, and savage competition. She claimed that the elimination of friction, while admirable in itself, had also resulted in the transformation of lovemaking from a passionate, complex, and meaningful

86

experience into a premeditated, cerebral, so-called civilized act based on carefully calculated compatibility. The problem, she said, was that the main character, an attractive woman, was a product of the type of education that championed the alleged superiority of science while condemning intimate relations as distracting, egotistical, and dangerous to global efficiency.

We could see Mount Hermon on the horizon, and she said she loved to ski. She wouldn't have traded the chance to do what she was doing for anything in the world, but the cherished tradition of semiannual family vacations in Europe was the one thing she was willing to admit she truly missed, the one thing she wished she hadn't been forced to put on hold for the duration of her service. She adored the Alps. And Paris. Not to mention Prague. Such a special city. But Italy was by far her favorite place. So much culture, so much history. And the clothes were gorgeous, simply gorgeous. Especially if you knew where to shop.

I told her I had never been to Prague, although my grandfather, in the spring of 1939, was hiding there from the Gestapo. Germany had invaded and annexed Czechoslovakia, and he managed to pretend, with the help of his professors, to be confined to the university hospital with an allegedly contagious disease. When it was clear that he had to flee, it was Adolf Eichmann, then in charge of Jewish emigration, who had inspected his papers, signed his passport, and allowed him to leave. Following the Velvet Revolution, my mother thought it would be a good idea to treat him to a trip to Europe. She thought it would be interesting for him, fifty years later, to revisit some of those old places. Prague, for example. He told her he preferred to stay at home. He had already seen Prague.

In a depraved city built on a magnetic field of liquid energy fueled by evil thoughts and deeds, those who were good had been exiled to an isolated, heavily guarded labyrinth, where they lived as prisoners. I saw the main character as a space-age Jesus: passive, submissive, repeatedly mocked, physically tortured. The encryption officer saw her as a confident, determined, resourceful liberator who defeated her tormentors and destroyed the cruel city. I said it was Jerusalem. She said it was Rome. I said that the main character was an animated paper doll given to fits of gratuitous wardrobe changes. She said she was portrayed as an unapologetic woman capable of concentrating on her own pleasure rather than a submissive object focused on satisfying others. I said that the female tyrant who ruled the city from her lavish and corrupt temple was the equivalent of the high priest. She said that the tyrant represented the emperor.

It was getting late. She folded the towels, put her clothes on, and drove us back to Tel Aviv. When we stopped for gas, a man approached us and said he admired her car. She thanked him, and he asked if it was for sale. His clothes were dirty, and he smelled. She smiled, and said no. He asked how much. She patted the hood and told him, in a slightly louder voice, that her car was not for sale. Twenty thousand dollars, he said. She laughed. Twenty-five, he said. She asked him why not thirty. Deal, he said. She laughed again, and told him that she only took cash. No problem, he said, and pulled a stack of banknotes from his pocket. He counted thirty thousand dollars and handed her the money. Wait, she said. No, he said, and told her that a deal was a deal. He had always wanted to own a two-seater. He pointed at his plumbing van, which was parked by the convenience store, and asked us to excuse him while he went to get a pen and paper. He trusted her completely, and he knew that the feeling was mutual, but things had to be done properly.

He wrote, on the back of an old brochure for faucets and flush valves, that the seller, in exchange for her vehicle, acknowledged receipt of the abovementioned amount, and that the buyer, having waived his right to inspect the vehicle, hereby agreed to purchase it in its current condition. He dated and signed it, then handed her his pen and told her she could keep it. His specialty was toilets and urinals, both domestic and commercial. He gave me an identical pen and said that if we ever needed his services, we could call or page him anytime, day or night. He also said that no additional authentication was required, but since I happened to witness this transfer of ownership, I could go ahead and add my name and signature to the impromptu bill of sale, right here, on the bottom, just in case. Then he asked if he could have the keys.

She said that she would have to give him the car tomorrow. Otherwise, how was she supposed to get home?

He said that he was sorry, but such an arrangement was not, to the best of his understanding, part of the deal.

Please, she said. She mentioned the fact that she was an army officer and promised to deliver the car, as soon as she could, directly to his home, or any other place of his choosing.

He said that he had also served in the army. He couldn't wait to feel the power of this beauty. But he would, out of the goodness of his heart, ask his assistant, who was waiting in the van, to drive us home.

She transferred the towels, along with the rest of her belongings, to the van, and we climbed in. Not again, the assistant said, and started the engine. We, the Jews, were very capricious. He couldn't tell if we were using pounds, shekels, or new shekels. The only thing, he said, that was eternal in this country was the dollar. The encryption officer said that she supposed that Muslims, whose ingenious calendar made sure that the spring months sometimes happened in the spring, sometimes in the summer, sometimes in the winter, and sometimes in the fall, were paragons of consistency. He said that he agreed. Personally, he was Catholic, from the village of Fassuta, home of Anton Shammas. I said that Anton Shammas, and this was just my unprofessional view, had written the most complex, most sophisticated, most memorable Hebrew novel of the modern age. She laughed and asked him if he had a cigarette. He drew a crumpled pack from his shirt pocket and said that he trusted my judgement, although personally, he hadn't read the book. She asked if I had sworn, at the end of my basic

89

training, loyalty to our defense forces with my hand on a copy of some work of fiction. I told her that soldiers who followed the Jewish commandments and abstained from taking vows were exempt from the requirement to swear an oath of allegiance. Instead, I had simply been asked to declare my willingness to abide by the rules of the army. Personally, he hadn't served in the army, but it was his opinion that if God had intended the Bible to be used as a verification document, he would have shaped it like an identity card, not like a book.

We spent the rest of the ride in silence. She smoked another cigarette. When the assistant dropped us off at the central bus station, she asked if I wanted to grab something to eat before we went our separate ways. She didn't care where. You choose, she said. I chose a typical Yemenite restaurant: cloudy fluorescent lights, small plastic tables, heavy silverware. The food, limited variations on dough and butter, some sweet, some traditionally spiced, was good. She said she didn't know if she should share this, but after everything we had been through today, she felt she could confide in me. She had gone out with a man: their first and only date. A movie, then a coffee shop, where they sat and talked for hours. And then, because neither of them was tired, and because young and carefree people oblivious to immediate threats always viewed our territorial waters as something romantic: a late-night walk by the sea. Nobody else was around, and they sat on the beach and kissed. He inserted his hand into the front of her pants, and she said: Don't. He said: Such an old line. She told him she was afraid that a grain of sand might get in there and grow into a pearl. He said: I'll be careful. She said: Such an old line. And that was it.

It was getting late. She shook my hand, an official gesture that somehow struck me as sincere, and said that she would see me tomorrow.

The following morning, on the base, she asked my commanding officer if she knew that I had a religious past. She produced a compact mirror from her purse, touched her face and neck, and said she should have been more careful in the sun. She put the mirror away and told my commanding officer that it was probably because of my orthodox background that I had averted my eyes when exposed, inadvertently, to her nakedness. Not that she would have ever felt embarrassed, but I had, she explained to my commanding officer, acted very sweetly. My commanding officer raised an eyebrow.

In my mind, the encryption officer sat at home, long after her return to the division, and constructed, in her imagination, the elaborate fantasies that my commanding officer and I had invented in our heads. In these fantasies, which she transcribed and translated into a series of short stories, she aroused my commanding officer physically, me intellectually. And when I called her on the phone, in my mind, she said that she was busy. Books took time, she said, and even though it looked like she was doing nothing, she had a full schedule. She said that according to the Talmud, God himself spent the first three hours of every day studying the Torah. According to the Zohar, God was very fond of the work of serious, talented, innovative scholars of the Bible and the Oral Law. The work of such scholars soared all the way to heaven, where God would sit and read it.

Kate Flannery

Monument Valley and *The Man of the West*

I married a Man of the West. He stayed around for about forty years then rode into the sunset with another woman who was the age of our daughter.

As a boy, he grew up in the San Fernando Valley in the 1950s when the place was shaking off its farmland dust and experiencing a post-war building boom. A few pockets of small, backyard ranches and farms still remained, however, when the boy was a child.

The boy grew up next door to one of those backyard ranches where a man named "Red" Morgan lived. Red broke and trained horses for the movies. The boy could hear the horses whinny and call to each other at night as he went to sleep. He dreamed of them. Red taught his horses to jump over boulders, down into deep ravines and into fast rivers and then up the steep banks on the other side. Sometimes he taught them to jump off cliffs.

The Wild West, it seemed, where all the cowboys' horses lived, was right next door to the boy, and Red had stories to tell about it all. The boy thought that Red's best stories were about Monument Valley. The boy knew how big the buttes and pinnacles of the place were, fashioned over millions of years, because he saw how they made John Wayne look small by comparison, even when riding his horse, Banner. Red also told a few stories about his horses traveling to Chatsworth for filming TV westerns, and the boy was known to hitch rides frequently to see "Lone Ranger Rock" whenever he had a chance. It was the place where Clayton Moore called out to his horse to ride out for justice.

Through all of it, the boy maintained a dream of visiting Monument Valley some day and seeing where John Wayne rode his horse out for justice in *Fort Apache, She Wore a Yellow Ribbon* and *The Searchers*.

Red never mentioned that the orchestra blaring Max Steiner's music in the movies wasn't out there too in Monument Valley when John Ford was filming his movies. Red never talked about the way the crews mistreated his horses. And he didn't describe details like the actors sweltering in the dust-filled heat without much shelter and without any flush toilets. The old men who made the movies in Monument Valley thought the place was noble, worthy of the men who rode through it. And so, they served up their stories on celluloid platters for young boys to consume.

The boy learned that Men of the West took land because they could, because the land belonged to those who could hold on to it. The Men did not see that they were not "human beings," as the Navajo people who lived near Monument Valley described themselves. Those human beings believed the place belonged to them. From the beginning. But Red never mentioned that either.

And as the boy became a Young Man, he would ride on his motorcycle through Monument Valley and beyond. He rode to Civil War battlefields and wept for the bravery and nobility of the soldiers who died there. And he read poetry and pondered important ideas like Truth and Beauty and Honor. He called those ideas testaments to the civilization of The West. The Young Man was becoming a philosopher.

And after studying about those enduring things, The Man became an educator and began to teach them to young men at universities and other places of learning. He made friends with men who taught the same things and together they grew to know other movies that spoke of the West's enduring monuments, movies like *Red River* and *The Man Who Shot Liberty Valance*.

I listened to and loved the talk and watched the movies too and helped pass the stories on to our child. All the young men and their teachers would gather in our home and read more poetry and talk more about important things they had learned and taught together. And they would sit in a circle outside as the sun was setting and drink beer and brandy and smoke cigars and talk about Aristotle and

Churchill and John Wayne and physical prowess and manliness and the enduring truths of civilization. They talked about The West.

But the Man's and my daughter was never allowed to ask questions at these gatherings; she remembers only the smell of stale beer and old smoke, what was left behind after everyone had left.

And now, after thinking about my daughter's questions and having dared to ask them as my own in these gatherings, I too know those things that are left behind.

The Man rode a 1976 Honda Goldwing as he grew older—an understated classic. Not flashy. No saddle bags. After all, a Man of the West is essentially a modest man who moves freely without encumbrances. A Man with no ego and disdainful of the helmet that California requires while a Man is riding the roads.

But as he turned into an old Man, he was afraid that he had lost something. He wondered if it was something of Beauty and Honor that he had spent his time and his dreams on during his 70 years as a Man of the West, and so he left his family—his wife and his daughter—and searched again in Monument Valley. No matter how hard he searched, he found only emptiness.

He did not see the place's ageless grace, its enduring truth.

Suzanne Greenberg

Offering

When my sister, Marla, comes to visit, we decide to take a hike to the Hollywood sign. She lived here two decades ago when we were both in our early twenties. We were even roommates for a year, sharing a sun-filled bedroom with splintery wood floors on the second level of a pink four-plex in not-quite Silverlake. When Marla decided to move to the valley to be closer to the industry, specifically closer to the semi-abandoned warehouse buildings where she often auditioned, I edged closer to the westside.

You might remember her as the pretty but annoying neighbor on any number of short-lived television sitcoms, the kind of shows they don' t make anymore. She was the one who knocked at the door carrying a lemon cake or oatmeal cookies or a peach pie to welcome the new neighbors. And then it turned out the cake tasted like dandruff or the cookies crumbled like sawdust or the pie was store bought and stale, or she dropped it, the gelled peaches spreading like mold on the newly installed carpet.

She even had a few movie roles, mostly doing background work as she was careful to call it. She was quick to remind you if you met her at a party that there was nothing extra about any of it.

My sister used to be the kind of elegantly undernourished girl who could show up late at a party sulking and leave early with the sexiest guy there. I watched Marla do this so many times I stopped going out with her, even with the promise of free alcohol and food. Instead, I stuck a frozen Lean Cuisine in the microwave and stayed home and studied for the bar exam. Which is not easy to pass, by the way, in California.

Now my sister lives in the desert with her husband, Don. He had a few decent roles as a drugged-out house painter and an empathetic bartender, but he found his real niche playing cowboys in movies. Sometimes he still does, filming outside of Lone Pine or in the scrubs of Joshua Tree. Mostly, he's retired now even though he's not yet fifty. If you ran into him in line at Ralph's or El Pollo Loco, you'd recognize his profile and wonder where you'd seen him.

My sister met him at one of the parties after I stopped going with her. She went home with him and in the morning walked into our apartment, put on a new pot of coffee and ran a shower as if her life hadn't changed one bit. He hounded her for weeks after that until she let him take her out on a real date. He picked her up on his motorcycle, but he may as well have been riding a quarter horse to our Silverlake adjacent four-plex. I'm not the easily swayed type, but I'd be lying if I didn't say I felt something buckle inside of me when he walked up our stairwell with a hand gripped tight around a bunch of white daisies.

They live in a trailer on the edge of a lot where they're building their dream home. I haven't been out there for months, but last Christmas when I visited, the house was still mostly just poured cement, a few 2 by 4s poking out. Don drew the rooms in chalk for me, and I walked through them as reverently as possible while he described the layout. I tried not to watch him move. His shoulders, his back, all of it impossible. "The atrium will be two floors high," he said, looking up at a flat blue sky.

Now I follow my sister up a hill. We originally parked in Beachwood Canyon only to find that trail closed behind a locked iron gate and had to compete for parking in Griffith Park to hike a longer, more populated trail. Star Waggons had taken over a chunk of the lots. Of course they had. Running into filming was unavoidable here.

My sister was furious I didn't know the Hollyridge trail was closed. "Jesus, it's been closed almost two years," she said more than once as we drove away and she typed furiously into her phone, figuring out where we should go. "You're the one who lives here. You should have known."

"It's not like I go hiking every day," I said. "I do have a job."

"Whatever," she said.

My job as an entertainment lawyer is of little interest to Marla now that she's left the industry. I have plenty of gossip, some even about A listers, but I'm not allowed to share it. Attorney/client privilege. Still, I used to tell Marla. I wouldn't give her names, just a first initial, and sometimes I even made that up, but we would open a bottle of something pricey, and if Don were there, I was suddenly the one who commanded the attention, not my glamorous little sister. Now I may as well work at Rite Aid as far as Marla's concerned.

We're half-way up the trail, and she's still angry. Marla's stomping on rocks, and I'm doing my best to keep up. She's no longer razor thin. Her butt is pushing out against her yoga pants, and I can see the seam pulling open at the middle. Her hair is in a high ponytail. Despite the weight gain, the truth is, she looks more like an irritated curvy teenager than the 42-year-old she is. My own hair is short and thin. The last stylist I saw highlighted it strategically and cut it in layers that were supposed to make it look fuller, but instead it looks wilted, with random swatches of color as if I were deciding on wall paint for my kitchen.

I feel the top of my head burning. Driving here and parking took another forty-five minutes and that translated into ten more degrees. Marla was so quick to get out of the car and start hiking, I left my hat and sunglasses behind trying to keep up with her, and now I try to keep my gaze low as if that will protect me from sunburn.

When Marla stops, I think it's because she's finally decided to wait for me. Maybe she's not mad anymore or she wants to talk. I still don't know why she's visiting me. All she said is she wanted to go hiking, and I took a Friday off to give us a long weekend together. Maybe we'd go to the beach on Saturday, I thought, the farmer's market on Sunday. I'd treat her like company instead of competition. Weren't we too old to compare lives?

I heard my phone beeping in my back pocket as we started out up the trail, but it's silent now, not because my work has stopped trying to get in touch with me despite my day off, but because no one has reception up here. The silence is more startling to me than the constant pings.

We are all stopped, not just Marla and me. A group of three girls wearing running shorts and orange Pepperdine tee shirts cut off at their midriffs have their phones out and are taking photos of something ahead on them. "I think that's him," one of them says.

"Fuck yes!" another says.

A small crowd of hikers has formed now, tourists with fancy folding hiking sticks, two men walking their dogs on tight leashes. I assume the men are partners because of their matching dogs, a large, frightening breed people are always calling intelligent. German Shepherds maybe. I am not an animal person. I once took care of a colleague's cat for the weekend when I was new at my firm and afraid of saying no and dry-heaved every time I scooped out the kitty litter.

Temporary medal fences are blocking the rest of the trail. "Oh, Jesus Christ. Now what," Marla says, but she's looking too.

I listen to the Pepperdine girls talking and find out they've come up here to watch a scene from a movie being filmed, hoping to catch a glance of its star. They have been doing detective work online, tracking this down, apparently arguing about the exact location. One of them says, "See, I told you I was right."

We don't represent him, but I've heard the actor's name muttered in our office. Someone is after him, has been talking to his manager. He's only twenty-two, but he's big, already being compared to Tom Cruise, Brad Pitt, Leonardo DiCaprio.

He is hiking up the trail in front of us, the one we're not allowed on, bundled up in a down jacket despite the heat, a rifle slung over his shoulder, walking toward a camera and a huge, mop-like mic.

"He's so hot," one of the Pepperdine girls says.

"OMG," another one adds.

"He can shoot me anytime," the third one says.

They are all blond and slim and anywhere but here, where they look like nearly everyone else, they might be mistaken for budding movie stars themselves.

"Do you have any idea who I am?" Marla says to them.

"Should we?" one of them says, turning away from the filming and wrinkling up her freckled nose in a way her boyfriend probably finds adorable.

Marla stares at her for a so long, I feel my heart start to pound. She is capable, my sister, in truth, of saying almost anything. "Not really," Marla says. "Come on, Colleen. Let's get out of here."

Walking down the hill, Marla is slower, and I have to measure my own stride to her pace. "It was only a matter of time," she says.

"What was?" I say.

"Come on. Everyone knew it was only a matter of time."

And suddenly I do know. Don. I am not proud of my reaction. But here it is: I think, why didn't I sleep with him if he was going to cheat on my sister anyway? It may just as well have been me.

"A fucking hostess at some scumball restaurant in Twenty Nine Palms."

"Oh, I'm sorry, Marla," I say, and now that I've gotten ahold of myself, I am.

"Maybe I'll move back in with you," she says. "Just like the old days. Remember how much fun we had."

I'm searching for an answer that doesn't come when we hear the gunshot. Our hero has been shot at while hiking, or maybe he's shot someone. Or shot at a bird or a deer or a rattlesnake. Yes, probably a rattlesnake. They wouldn't even

99

have to import one—these hills are filled with them—but I'm sure they did.

One of the dogs that had been held so tightly on its leash is off and running past us, its leash dragging behind it. I push Marla out of the way. We are in the scrub on the side of the trail when the dog's owner comes running after him. "Shit!" he is screaming. "Get back here, Henry."

Marla starts laughing first, and then I'm laughing, too. "That poor dog," I say. "That poor man. We're being mean."

"You were never mean," Marla says. "I'm the mean one."

I think about telling Marla something mean about myself, how sometimes I go home with men the way she used to. I meet them at bars or online. I don't want anything that lasts. I like my apartment with its clean surfaces and can't imagine what a man's discarded socks and emptied pockets would add to my life. But I don't tell Marla any of this. I also don't tell her about the mammogram I had three years ago that required further monitoring and now how I have to schedule special appointments every year where the woman who checks me in smiles with practiced pity. We haven't been that kind of sisters, and it seems too late to become that now.

Our parents, who live in Danville, a bay area suburb people afraid of San Francisco move to when they have children, have stopped hinting about grandchildren. We're too old now. I think about how at least Marla is married and I'm a lawyer, how our parents have that. But maybe Marla will be divorced and they'll just have the part about me to remind themselves they didn't fail and have something to talk about at dinner parties. But instead of feeling victorious, I just feel sad.

Marla and I walk together back down the trail the rest of the way without talking, my phone now beeping again in my back pocket. I don't have to tell Marla that she can't live with me, despite my spare bedroom with the queen bed with the good mattress. All I have to do is pretend she didn't ask.

"Maybe you two can work it out," I say.

"I doubt it," she says. "Come on," she says. Marla pulls me over to a Star Waggon where they have set out a buffet of food, salads, and salami and olives and cheese and fruit for the crew and cast. "Just play along," she says. "Don't say anything."

Marla smiles her still dazzling smile at a man lining up water bottles, and we grab thick plastic plates and load them up. Spilled food from our plates trails behind us as we navigate through cars back to ours.

When we hear the brakes squeal in the road at the far end of the parking lot, Marla drops her plate and grips the top of my arm so tightly, she makes a bruise that will last for days after she drives back to her trailer in the desert. We hear the barks and screams and don't have to see anything to know the man whose dog escaped is bent over in the road next to the parking lot crying.

"I can't look," she says.

"Let's not," I say.

"We should help," Marla says.

"What could we do," I say, a statement, not a question.

My sister loosens her grip on my arm and I reach for her hand as if we are eight and six again, instead of the disappointing adult cowards we have become. I used to walk her home from school this way, her fingers linked through mine.

Despite myself, I turn and look in the direction where the dog has been hit. I see the man carrying it now in a blanket someone must have given him. He is walking through the parking lot holding the covered dog out in front of him like some kind of offering, the other man and his dog taut on his leash following behind. I'm not sure but I think I can hear him crying from here, or maybe it's just a red fox off in the hills somewhere screaming out in urgent primal longing.

Faith Shearin

On the Shore

Jane's husband, Max, died on the first day of November and afterwards, while weeping in the dim winter of her living room and watching her son's betta fish swim through a castle in a dirty aquarium, she realized she must survive the holidays. She watched the fish fan his burgundy tail beside a miniature shipwreck while thinking of how much she dreaded Thanksgiving, when the windowless aisles of the Food Lion became impassable; she sprinkled fish food along the surface of the aquarium and thought of how she dreaded Christmas with its throbbing lights and swampy eggnog; she watched the fish ascend to the surface of the tank, his mouth opening to each red pellet, while thinking of how she dreaded New Year's Eve, during which her neighbors set off sparklers, and drank champagne, and their balloons escaped: strings entangled in trees while their bright orbs—full of helium and hope—went on trying to rise. Worst of all, there was January 17, Max's birthday: a day Jane thought should be erased from all calendars. Jane's son, Sam, had returned from college that afternoon, by train: unshaven, in a plume of smoke, with a single overstuffed backpack, and he would remain at home until late January; the two of them drifted through the darkness like unmoored boats.

"Should we buy a turkey?" Jane asked Sam the day before Thanksgiving.

"Fuck, no," Sam said, "Why would we do that? We can barely eat."

The first Thanksgiving Max did not live to see was blustery and gray; a cold wind blew from the east. Jane and Sam ate the foods that had arrived on their doorstep before the funeral: cheeses and summer sausages; pears wrapped in tissue paper, buried in boxes that reminded Jane of coffins; cookies ruined by raisins. Sam suggested that they watch horror movies on the big TV in the living room and Jane

102

agreed, popping a bowl of popcorn with a noisy air popping machine an aunt had given to her at a bridal shower twenty-four years before; Jane thought of this aunt: still alive in her ranch home in North Carolina, despite her diabetes and gout, while Max had vanished into the silent rafters of the afterlife.

Sam connected a DVD player to the TV and he and Jane began by watching *The Blob:* the story of a shapeless Jell-O-like substance that oozed through a Pennsylvania town, consuming all the citizens in its path: an auto mechanic, teenagers dancing around a bonfire on a beach, shoppers roaming the aisles of a department store. Jane found herself rooting for the blob and its appetites; she felt a certain excitement each time it hovered, gelatinously, at the edge of ordinary life.

They watched a pert blonde, Marion, check into Norman Bates' roadside hotel and decide to take a shower.

"This woman should *not* take a shower," Jane said.

"Don't you love the way Hitchcock filmed this scene?" Sam said, as a disembodied hand with a knife began stabbing.

"The blood is actually Hershey's chocolate syrup," Jane said.

"My film professor told me," Sam said.

They watched *Jaws*, in which attractive young people were continuously boating or swimming, until ominous music began to play and someone yelled: *Look out, a shark!* The sharks were ubiquitous, and toothy, and perpetually starved. Sam cast a shadowy aquatic creature against the wall with his left hand and, using the thumb of his right, created a fin; he made a low, threatening sound at the back of his throat. Jane began to feel more like herself during their movie marathon; it was easy to pretend Sam was a few years younger, and Max was somewhere upstairs, or about to return from a business trip; she liked the way her own story fell away and was replaced by another; she liked comparing her own plight to the plight of characters in horror films.

In *Alien*, Jane and Sam watched a space merchant vessel receive a distress call from a distant moon where a submerged ship contained an eerie chamber filled with eggs. Jane took out her knitting, and Sam opened a bag of pistachio nuts too forcefully, their shells cascading over the coffee table onto the wood floor; in their old life, one of them would have found the broom and swept up the fallen shells, but, for a reason Jane could not articulate, death made housework impossible. Jane and Sam watched as a captain, executive officer, and navigator decided to investigate the drowned spacecraft and its odd cargo.

"This guy should not be so curious," Sam said when the officer leaned over an egg and the parasite inside latched onto his head.

"People in horror films are always curious," Jane said.
"Dad hated horror films," Sam said.
"They gave him nightmares," Jane agreed.

At dusk Jane remembered their dachshund, Paper, required a walk. Sam found him upstairs, his long snout tucked under Max's desk, where he had been hoarding things: a toothbrush, a tissue he had shredded, delicately, with his front teeth, a pair of Jane's reading glasses, one of Max's tennis shoes. Jane and Sam walked together, their silhouettes made bulky by coats, their hands encased in mittens. Sam allowed Paper to choose the direction he preferred and this was most often a street named *Ladyslipper* with street lamps and Victorian houses; Paper favored this route because it offered an array of dogs behind invisible fences: two pugs, one dark, one light, who barked in unison, the light one hopping excitedly on top of the darker one; then, several houses later, an elegant Alaskan husky with human eyes who wagged his white tail in circles; across the street from the husky, a bassett hound, Romeo, dressed in drooping, oversized skin, who slept at the end of a leash, attached to a stake, in front of a dog house. Romeo was Paper's friend and they touched noses lightly in the twilight, before Jane and Sam turned back towards the meadow that had once been a farm, and crossed over the rail trail, heading home. As they walked, Jane tried not to look into the houses of her neighbors where families sat in front of flickering fireplaces or lingered at tables heaped with the remains of feasts: carcasses, casseroles, half-eaten pumpkin pies.

In the weeks since Max's death, Jane had spent a few hours of her insomnia adding up credit card bills; Jane and Max had always paid more attention to dreams than wealth and this had seemed adventurous when Max was alive but now, alone, Jane was afraid. When she and Max had decided she should quit teaching to focus on her paintings and stay home with Sam—after all, the childcare cost nearly as much as her salary—they had not also considered what would happen if Max died suddenly of a heart attack at 48 and no one wanted to hire Jane. Once Max's life insurance gave out Jane knew she and Sam would need to leave this gentle neighborhood full of professors for some other and, already, she felt like a visitor or a ghost; she did not know if she could find a job teaching art at the age of 49, or if she could even answer an interview question without sweating to death, and, if she could not, she would make so little money as a cashier, or waitress, or secretary she imagined she would grow old in a back room of her sister's house in Chicago. When she ate her sandwich at the park on Wednesdays, on the way to the grocery store, Jane watched a freckled homeless woman, with hair as long and wild as her own, pushing a grocery cart to a bench where pigeons gathered; she noticed this woman's hands, which trembled as she reached into a bag of bread; she noticed the contents of the woman's cart: soda cans, a coat, a sleeping bag, a stack of Agatha Christie novels. Sometimes the homeless woman began conversations with invisible people, and Jane understood this now that Max was ethereal but still seemed to drift through all the drafty rooms of her house, setting off

105

fire alarms or moving the dial on her radio. Once, after the homeless woman pushed her cart down Main Street and into the yard of the Emily Dickinson Museum, Jane found herself beside a group of young housewives with toddlers, and, while watching them, she remembered all the places she and Sam had travelled together when he was small: art classes where Sam made unrecognizable sculptures from Play-Doh, music classes where mothers and children gathered around an old Australian man with a guitar and clapped and sang about Waltzing Matilda and Kookaburras, swimming classes in which mothers were asked to recite *Humpty Dumpty* while dunking their children in a hot salt water pool. (She had quit taking Sam to this last one when she found him reciting nursery rhymes while drowning his plastic superheroes in the bathtub.) Jane remembered how, for several years after Sam was born, everything had seemed new again because it was new to Sam: sand, snow, chocolate, earthworms, trees. In her mind, Jane measured the distance between the young housewives and the woman surrounded by pigeons.

At the library, the day before Sam returned from college, Jane had opened a fragile, historic book about early Massachusetts widow auctions; she read about the early 1600s when women like Jane were sold as slaves to wealthy New England families, their value decreasing as they aged; the book referred to women over forty-five as *feeble* and *undesirable for marriage*; she lingered over a passage about a particularly angry widow in Deerfield, also named Jane, who cried out *for shame* when she was placed on an auction block. In a phone meeting with an administrator in Max's old office the week after he died, Jane realized her health insurance— which had been attached to Max's job—had become unaffordable.

"You could *COBRA* the insurance," the administrator explained, "but that would cost around a thousand dollars a month."

Jane pictured an actual cobra, slithering.

"What do *you* do?" the administrator asked, hopefully. "Maybe you can access a plan through *your* employer?"

"I'm a housewife," Jane replied; then she realized that no one is a housewife if they don't have a husband, "Or, I guess, I'm unemployed?"

Jane's phone vibrated and she paused to examine it; the air around her grew colder in the inky darkness. She pulled off a mitten to touch her text messages and the mitten vanished. Maybe it had fallen from her pocket into a snowbank? Jane turned back, scanning the ground beneath a street lamp, the fingers of her right hand growing numb; she searched the darkness, which reminded her of the heavy darkness at the bottom of the sea. After a few minutes she gave up, exhausted by gravity and by all the things in the world that were fallen or hidden; she realized she had wasted years of her life searching for lost objects or waiting for red lights to change. Instead, Jane began searching for Paper's low, pointy profile and Sam's straight back and mass of curls; she turned towards the road at the edge of the meadow but found herself alone, among a confusion of tire tracks and footprints, the night starless; she heard the rush of trucks in the distance. Jane walked fast, then faster, her other mitten slipping out of her pocket, her eyes blurring.

"Mom," Sam called from the front porch of the house where he and Paper waited beside the mailbox: the exact place where, three weeks before, Jane had received a Federal Express envelope stuffed with death certificates, each one the size and shape of a diploma, as if Max had graduated to some other world by developing *hyperlipidemia* and *biventricular valve failure*. On each certificate, it seemed to Jane that Max's life had been flattened: reduced to times and dates.

Paper let out a short, low bark.

"Sorry I lost you," Jane said, wiping her eyes with the sleeve of her coat, "I got a text from your grandmother."

"What did she say?" Sam asked.

"She wonders if we're eating turkey," Jane said.

"Paper was distracted by a squirrel," Sam said.

"Someone should make a horror film about squirrels," Jane said.

Jane put the tea kettle on the stove and Sam found a puzzle on the bookshelf; they cleared off the kitchen table and began sorting the pieces of van Gogh's *Wheatfield with Crows*. Jane remembered buying this puzzle on a trip with Sam and Max to the Smithsonian when Sam was so small that he ran through all the polished corridors and tried to touch a Degas sculpture of a dancer with a ponytail; before Jane could stop him, he had wrapped his tiny hand around one of the dancer's ballet shoes and two guards hurried from the corners of the room. Max, who had been walking some distance behind, paused to examine a Chagall painting and pretended not to know them.

Afterwards, in a courtyard with cafe tables and a fountain, Max rearranged his chicken salad. "Remind me why we're chasing a three-year-old through an art museum?" he asked.

"It's educational?" Jane had said.

The art museum had been Jane's idea.

On this same trip they had stopped in Alexandria to visit a couple they'd known in college, Amy and Dave, and Sam spent the evening catching fireflies in a Mason jar, at the edge of a freshly mown lawn, with Amy and Dave's two tiny curly-haired daughters, who wore no pants.

"We're potty training," Amy told Jane.

"The pediatrician gave Amy a book," Dave said, his brow furrowed as he lit a barbecue grill.

"If those children are potty trained," Max said to Jane the next morning, in their car, after they had waved goodbye to Amy and Dave and Sam had fallen asleep in his car seat, Cheerios stuck to the front of his shirt, "then I'm a jet pilot."

"It was a little distracting," Jane said, "all that child nudity."

"One of them *peed* on me," Max said.

"When?" Jane asked.

"When Amy was showing you the garden," Max said.

"Did Dave notice?" Amy asked.

"He apologized," Max said, "I think he's afraid of Amy and the whole thing is definitely *her* idea."

"I wonder what kind of book the pediatrician gave her?" Jane said.

There were so many childrearing books and, during those first years, Jane always had one on her bedside table: books that suggested mothers should leave their babies screaming alone in cribs so they could learn to self-soothe; books that insisted mothers should sleep with their babies pressed against them so they could learn warmth and kindness; books that urged mothers to return to work, and books that warned that a lack of steady maternal presence would lead to improper attachment and developmental delays.

Jane could remember the exact blue of the sky that morning between Alexandria and Baltimore, could remember the seafood she and Max ate in the stone downtown of Ellicott City where they stopped to see the oldest surviving train station; they had stepped inside a long room full of wooden benches to examine photos of passengers from the past in black coats and hats with steamer trunks, and back there, in the balmy September weather of 2003, Jane continued ordering clam chowder in a cup and carrying it through the cobblestone streets, with Sam in a stroller, Max's hand on the small of her back.

"Isn't this the last thing van Gogh ever painted?" Sam asked, while piecing together a crow.

"No one seems to know which painting was his last," Jane said, "At least that's what I was told in art history class."

"They agree that he went crazy," Sam said.

"But they can't agree on the exact *nature* of his insanity," Jane said.

109

In a used bookstore full of dust and cats, a place where books rose in unsorted piles as tall as trees, Sam found a volume full of hiking trails that led through four ghost towns at the edge of the Quabbin Reservoir.

"I think we should go hiking in one of these towns tomorrow," he announced on Christmas Eve, when he and Jane were sitting in the living room in the blue, treeless twilight; Sam had opened a map that showed the roads of the towns that had been drowned to create the reservoir so the people of Boston could have enough to drink. He and Jane were watching his betta fish make a bubble nest amid algae at the corner of the aquarium; Jane thought of how the fish was suspended, like Max, in some wordless, submerged world; she thought of how a male betta fish must live alone because he is prone to fighting; sometimes, in the right light, this fish had caught a glimpse of himself in the aquarium glass and Jane had seen how he paced and flared.

Jane and Sam had not bought lights, or gifts, and neither of them had eaten a proper meal that day except for a plate of scrambled eggs at noon. It was amazing, really, how the rest of the world hurried to classes and jobs and appointments. Outside, a skeletal branch scratched the window behind the couch; dishes were stacked in the sink, and pistachio shells had gathered beneath the coffee table, each one like a miniature boat that had run aground; Paper began scratching and nibbling a spot on his leg. It seemed to Jane that she was the opposite of an adult for she could not remember how to structure a day or plan for the future; she didn't care if the oil was changed in the car or if the sheets on her bed were clean.

"Are you sure?" Jane asked Sam, "Isn't it supposed to be cold?"

"We have coats," Sam said.

On Christmas Day, while their neighbors tore open gifts in front of glowing trees, Jane and Sam packed peanut butter and jelly sandwiches, loaded the station wagon, and drove twenty minutes to the north, to the remains of the drowned town of Dana. Jane was at the wheel, and Paper balanced beside her, on top of the drink holder, his short legs tucked under him, his slender nose pointed forward; Sam was in the passenger seat with a map unfolded in his lap, where Max had often sat. Sam's beard had come in fully now and his face, in the weeks since his father died, had grown older. When they arrived, Sam opened his map and led Jane and Paper down a winding dirt road to a town square where they discovered the stone foundation of a schoolhouse which was now full of snow instead of children; they found the cellar of a farmhouse where a broken oven from the 1930s had filled with dirt and finches; they visited the remains of a country store with a porch where villagers had once gathered to buy sugar and exchange gossip; Jane and Sam and Paper stood inside the stone outline of a church where there had once been pews and music and sermons; Paper stuffed his slender nose down a hole. They found themselves beside a grove of low, crooked apple trees, each one wizened and hunched. Sam was good at reading an old-fashioned map, something Max had taught him to do on their family hiking trips.

"You won't always have a GPS," Max had warned, and, of course, this was true.

Jane and Sam and Paper hiked down a dirt road that had once run through the center of Dana's downtown until it disappeared under water.

"There was a midnight ball," Sam read to Jane from the history book he'd brought along, "on the last night that Dana was an incorporated town, before the flooding for the reservoir began."

"The people of Boston must have been very thirsty," Jane said, imagining how many villagers had left behind their familiar acres. "Did they dance?"

"What?" Sam said.

"At the midnight ball," Jane said, "Did people dance?"

"It doesn't say," Sam said.

Jane peered into the reservoir which was full of the sunken remains of villagers' lives: the trees they had once climbed or carved with initials, the hillsides where they had gone sledding, the stone foundations of houses where schools of fish now flicked their gauzy tails; surely, somewhere down there, doors led to sunken bedrooms and kitchens, to streets where people had laughed or kissed. She opened the backpack she had been carrying, and unfolded a blanket, and sat down with her son, and her dog, and they picnicked on the shore where the terrestrial town gave way to the submerged town; they pulled their coats tight around them and ate beneath a maple tree, in the shade where all the old roads paused for a moment before they drowned.

Brian Walter

Snow Day

A couple of days before he entered the hospital where he would, a few months later, die while awaiting a heart transplant that never came, my father took what would be his last ride up into the mountains. I had been in Oregon for about a week during the Christmas holidays, and this was my final day with my parents; I suggested we make good use of the gleaming red SUV the rental agency had unexpectedly tendered me by going for a drive up old state route 20 into the western slopes of the Cascades. The forecast called for snow, with several inches expected in the mountains, and the first pellets were already dotting the windows as we finished breakfast. Dad tried not to look fearful at the prospect of being so far away from a hospital, tried to focus only on the pleasure of spending this last day with his son enjoying the kind of winter-beatified scenery that he had always praised so confidently: a simple means of escape from the complicated disappointments of his life. I reminded him of the time—this was an old favorite story—he'd arranged a special birthday gift outing for his own father decades before on a snowy day a continent away in his hometown of Perry, Ohio. He smiled slowly in response, assenting finally to the idea, but his apprehension was still palpable.

It had not been an easy visit. At least since his most recent heart attack the previous spring, Dad had been pretty much an invalid. Mom had always managed their home life carefully, keeping the place spic-and-span for her neat-freak husband, cooking all the meals, washing all the dishes and clothes, shopping for the groceries, and so on, but for some time now, she had also had to take over his household tasks: handling all the money, writing out the bills, taking out the garbage, attending to the yard, and, to her considerable initial distress, driving the car everywhere they went, something that Dad had always done. Then there were the many additional cares that had fallen to her lot as the result

113

of his precarious condition: setting up all of the medical and legal appointments, managing the mountain of pills he had to ingest daily, monitoring his diet, helping him get dressed, checking on him in the bathroom—he spent a lot of time in there because he was not, under any circumstances, to strain himself during bowel movements—and fetching extra blankets for him when he sat down in his easy chair, as his severely weakened heart no longer pumped enough blood to keep him warm even at normal indoor temperatures. That was yet another source of vague humiliation for my father, whose inner fires had always allowed him to complain manfully of being too warm in almost any environment.

My younger sister had moved out of their home and into her marriage some six years earlier, but now Mom had another child to take care of, fifty-five years old and as delicately balanced as the touchiest, most emotionally fragile kindergartener. Determined though he was to rise to the occasion of his grandiloquent son's visit, Dad had never looked worse, as gaunt and frail as an angry widow. Conversely, Mom had never looked better; she seemed to thrive on his dependency, finally the weighty member of the pair, anchoring her end of the teeter-totter to terra firma while he was stuck ignominiously aloft, legs dangling and useless, a human decoration debarred from all forms of control.

Not that she ever ceased playing her old traditional part. As always, she had packed plenty of snacks for what would turn out to be a three-hour ride and stationed herself in the middle of the back seat, ready to dote at the first sign of trouble. Dad had tried hard, as usual, to pretend it was no problem getting himself into the front passenger seat, which required him to pull himself up into the vehicle before settling in. Whenever he had to exert himself in his depleted state, he would close his lips and jut his chin slightly forward, mustering a hint of a smile to try to reassure his caretakers that it was really no strain. But his eyes still betrayed his despair, the labor of his breathing another loss he couldn't hide.

114

He was an unhappy passenger, checking the speedometer every few seconds, pumping imaginary brakes, looking over his own shoulder every time I changed lanes, estimating our catch-up speed and telling me immediately if I didn't move over when he thought I should to give a slower vehicle a wide enough berth. In a better world, I would have done a better job of ignoring his need to grasp at some sort of authority. But instead, as usual, I just responded with a favorite dig of passive aggression ("Relax, Dad") that was sure to pique him. Just as usual, he responded sarcastically ("Okay, okay, I'm relaxing") and then did anything but, leaning back rigidly into his seat, affecting some heavily-drawn breaths.

Leaving the small logging town of Lebanon, we soon passed through the even smaller logging town of Sweet Home, waiting for Mom to point out where, for so many years, her favorite aunt had lived, a block or two off the main drag. She was a sweet old white-haired woman whom the whole family had revered for her colorful, sentimental landscape paintings. When we would visit her house during my childhood, Dad and I had a little routine of going through the living room to admire her handiwork, Dad waiting until I had declared my favorite (a sunset lakescape as pristinely prettified as an excruciatingly sensitive ten-year-old could wish, stationed in the place of honor above the sofa) before he expressed his own preference for one of the less dramatically presented scenes tucked away in comparative obscurity down the hall (always first, however, acknowledging the legitimate appeal of my selection). She had died many years since by the time of this particular trip, and when Mom referred wistfully to her as we passed through town, Dad, for once, didn't chime in.

We were in no hurry, and there were not many other cars on the road, so we seldom broke 40 as we followed the curves up into the mountains. For a while, our route brought us frequent prospects of the Santiam River and some of its tributaries—narrower and shallower creeks of cold, noisy water, flowing over dark rocks worn smooth through the years and past the dead, blackened branches that had fallen from the trees still growing near their banks. I asked Dad if he remembered the time he had slipped and fallen in a creek near our house on Simonsen Road, the time when my older brother had accidentally caught a beaver in one of his traps. Dad remembered, and though he smiled automatically, the horror of that particular memory quickly erased the smile. He had wanted to set the poor creature free and tried several times to get near enough to spring the trap, but it was ferocious in its pain and terror, leaping and growling and spitting at him whenever he approached. In the end, Dad felt he had no choice but to dispatch it. He went back to the house and retrieved the ax, and all four of his children watched, goggle-eyed, as he inched near enough to bring the blunt edge of the blade down on the beaver's skull. It took him several swings to land a killing blow, and it was on the next-to-last one that he had slipped on the steep bank and slid down into the creek, frantically twisting to keep himself out of the reach of the now bleeding and woozy beaver. Dad was mad and muddy when he emerged, hating the executioner's part he still had to play. The next and last swing was augmented by his considerable anger, cracking the skull wide open. But the end of the killing ordeal only deepened the disgust, for when he and my brother opened up the body, we all recognized the kits inside the birth chamber, three or four little balls of brown fur almost fully-formed that Dad flicked out with the blade of the ax.

With Mom's ready acquiescence, we children had lionized Dad from the beginning, reassuring each other with stories of his athletic prowess as Perry High's star sprinter back in the day or with memories of the times he had wrestled all four of us at once and easily pinned us down for the win. In retrospect, it was clear that the heroic image we had fashioned had been propped up, in considerable part, by his almost constant absence from the domestic sphere, his work as a pastor or insurance salesman or exterminator apparently keeping him away from us most of the time and making him seem all the more grandiose in our eager minds.

116

The obvious pride he took in his children had always been magnified in return. Now though, what few triumphs life still afforded him happened mostly at the dinner table, playing cards or Scrabble or Trivial Pursuit with Mom. To step outdoors was to be humbled, even on an outing as quiet and outwardly peaceful as this snow day was proving.

By 11, Mom was ready to break out the sandwiches she'd made for us. That was also her signal to me that it was about time to start heading back, that we'd strayed far enough from the hospital, where Dad was on the transplant list that technically required him never to be more than an hour's drive away. So at the next turnout, with mixed feelings, I swung to the right, preparing to describe a comfortable U-turn into the opposite lane that would take us back west and north to the double-wide mobile home in the trailer park, the only piece of property Dad had ever owned. Dad looked out his window as I slowed down for the turn, watching in silence as the snow continued to fall, his face turned away from ours, a prisoner who knew his sentence was nigh.

Here is what didn't happen next. Abruptly, I stopped the vehicle and put it in park. Leaving the engine and heater on, I reached for my coat in the back seat. Dad's head whipped around, a surprised look on his face. In the back seat, Mom was trying hard to catch my eye with a look of fear and warning, her head shaking as unobtrusively as she could make it. Ignoring her, I hopped out, went around to the passenger side, grinned at Dad, and reached down into the snow with both hands to start forming a snowball. He grinned back. I didn't have gloves, but it didn't matter. I backed up a bit, tossing the snowball up and down lightly in my right hand.

More fictional license. Grinning all the more broadly as Mom, terrified, tried to keep him inside with her, Dad unbuckled his seat belt, opened the door, and stepped down gingerly into the snow, a solid white expanse on the far edge of the turnout, which itself was ringed by trees. The flakes were drifting down all around and onto us, catching in our eyelashes as we blinked, even laughing a bit at this unexpected bit of fun. He closed the door behind him and reached down into the snow to mold his own little emblem of masculine prowess, even as I shamelessly taunted him. No chance, old man. No chance at all.

Almost time for the catharsis (or nadir). I lobbed mine first, a bit to the right, where it landed on the steaming hood of the SUV. A few more chuckles. Then it was Dad's turn. I inched forward, still teasing the old codger, as he liked to refer to himself, giving him a better target. He wound up, ignoring Mom as she rolled down her window to plead with him, "Please don't, honey—please don't." It will be best if even she was grinning a bit by this point.

Dad let fly. I had made my plan. On impact, a little high up, just below the left collarbone, I dropped backward into the fresh powder behind me like I'd been shot, helpless and grinning in the impossible accuracy of my Dad's throw.

He awoke not to the sound of the wheelchair rolling across the fading yellow linoleum of the kitchen floor, nor even to his father's moist wheezings a moment later on the grey respirator box with the transparent breathing tube, some fourteen inches long and yellowed at the lip. Rather, it was the sound of water running into the bathroom sink just across the hall that coaxed him into consciousness. He left his eyes closed for a moment, conjuring the familiar scene. His mother would be removing her glasses, folding and setting them exactly halfway between the twin spigots (cold to the left, hot to the right), and then leaning over to wash her face with practiced hands. She would be wearing her mint-green robe cinched in a full knot at the waist (too thin, really, for February mornings in northern Ohio) and white slippers, open at the heel, a single three-inch wide band of furred material all that was holding them to the arches of her mottled feet. Her hair, now almost completely drifted in white, offered only the sparsest evidence of the near-black corona of curls it still bore in his memories, thinning visibly now too, but still brushed pat every night and parted, rather to the left of center, every morning. Turning off the water (with her eyes closed, of course), she would reach for the hand towel (never the larger bath towel on the farther side of the rack) and dry first beneath her left eye, then her right, before donning her glasses once more and heading downstairs to begin the ritual of breakfast. His mind followed her padded footsteps down the stairs, counting backward from eight down to one, listening for the slight scrape of her wedding ring against the knob of the bannister at the bottom, registering the first light tread.

Standing at the bedroom window now, cinching his own old robe (a sixteenth birthday gift so many years ago) a little snugly (to tell the truth) around his waist, he looked out at steel-gray, snow-heavy clouds mustering to the west. Downstairs, the living room cuckoo burst from its cage, insistently warning that the delivery of his birthday gift to his father was only an hour or two away. As a child, he would rush into the living room when the cuckoo commenced its routine, counting its abrupt protrusions carefully to make sure that the little wooden herald signaled the moment properly. Already obsessed with time, he had even begged for a wristwatch on his sixth birthday.

He soon descended the stairs in his mother's wake. When he was young, the members of the household broke the night's fast singly, whenever matitudinal habits summoned one from the labor of sleep, each taking a turn at the small, two-legged table anchored to the wall beside the stove. But with his visits growing much less frequent over the years, breakfast had become a communal affair whenever he did return home, his mother trying to smother the unmistakable awkwardness with scrambled eggs, pancakes, and sausage, her preacher son's favorite Sunday breakfast as a child. Arrayed around the large, nearly round dining room table, all three found the comforting old breakfast menu a helpful distraction from memories of the most painfully memorable time they had been together at that table, the time he had put a question to them that his parents would always (to the day they died) refuse to answer.

His father was still at the respirator when he entered the room, so he went over and laid a light hand on the thin, rigid left shoulder to wish him a happy birthday. Unable to speak since his stroke a few months earlier, his father nodded. He explained that they would need to hurry through their rather late breakfast to have enough time for the surprise gift he had arranged. His mother bustled breakfast to the table, urging father and son (who didn't much look like each other but who had usually pretended not to notice) to hurry and take their places.

After breakfast, awaiting the appointed hour, they all looked through a heavily-populated old photo album retrieved carefully from a closet shelf. It contained mostly black-and-white memories, bordered on all four sides in functional white, and marked with the month and year of development. From the yellowing pages, ill-disguised in a classic mid-century crewcut, he looked out innocently at his adult incarnation, in one shot brandishing a short fishing pole bent over at the upper end in obeisance to the hook fashionably caught in a line feeder half-way or more down the pole, white-and-red bobber (grey and greyer in the photo) stuck in forceful mid-kiss against the tip of the pole. In another shot, his hair long enough now to comb, he stood stiffly but proudly in the first new suit of teen-hood, pants that would be grey to any film topped by a speckled sport coat and cuffed by polished black loafers. His mother narrated the show, proudly sharing her reliquary. She particularly exclaimed over a close-up of him in the tell-tale mask of his then newly televised hero, poised to extinguish the full decade's worth of candles aflame in the frosting. That old black mask still hung from the upper left corner of the dresser mirror in his old room, its flimsy, brittle rubber band long ago replaced with a bit of kite-string that made the mask unwearable by any would-be silver bullet-slinger burdened with an adult-sized cranium, but much more sure in its mooring to the mirror. That morning, with a well-aimed gust, he had banished a skim of dust from the old hero's prop.

Paging through the album, his mother conjured names and dates as the magician does rabbits and paper flowers, navigating with almost alarming facility all of the cousins, aunts, uncles, nieces, nephews, grandparents, great-grandparents, friends, girlfriends, and casual acquaintances. She not only adorned the myriad subjects with their proper names, but also took pains to set their snapshots in flattering context. There's Aunt Ora, who made a lemon pie, topped with frothy meringue, when he had finally had his braces (that dental chastity belt) removed at the end of the ninth grade, a prize for him to enjoy as soon as his mouth stopped aching. And here's little Joey Bakken, his best friend until the fourth grade, who by age eight was forced to look at the world through lenses as thick as Coca-Cola bottles; didn't his family move away when his father, a preacher in a local Saturday-keeping congregation, suffered a falling out with his flock? Or what about this one of Mary Jane Lincoln, who looked so pretty there that night in her yellow-and-white print dress, left arm comfortably encircled in the elbow of that tallish Perry High senior, smiling now a bit wolfishly through an invisible hero's mask in his own spiffy Homecoming Dance get-up?

Each page flipped occasioned a new embroidery, a new pattern to be stitched up in neat idealization of the past. His father, bound to the two-wheeled throne of his debility, half-smiled through the show, sometimes glancing at the photo album, sometimes at the clock on the wood-paneled wall to his right, but most often out the window. It was snowing, flakes too tiny to be called white dissolving immediately when they hit the rough asphalt on the patch of Maple Street that could be seen.

His mother was just about to reach for the backup album she had also brought when the gift pulled into the driveway, rocking and bucking on the gravel. He noticed it a beat before his father and stepped to the window, leaving his father to strain this way and that in the cursed wheelchair in a vain attempt to see. Finally, his son moved aside, and he could see it: a 1911 Ford Model T Roadster, complete with mother-in-law's back seat left out in the cold, trying—with characteristically cantankerous humor—to complete the task of coming to a full stop. Its driver, obviously raised on the grainy fictions of an older silver screen, had decked himself out in full pilot's regalia: gloves, jacket, and cap in creaky chocolate-brown leather, rounded goggles somehow managing to emphasize the dark, full mustache (twirled to a point at the tips) standing at attention just below, scarf (yes, even a scarf) carefully wrapped once in the swashbuckler's manner over the collar of the jacket, its tasseled end wistfully awaiting a life-giving velocity that the old Flivver, game but never quick, could probably not bestow upon it. His father removed his gaze from the vehicle just long enough to look for a moment at his mother, who, having set aside both albums now, managed a smile.

The gift was his idea, of course. He had been raised on his father's stories of the old Roadster he'd bought on the cheap in the late 20s (when Henry Ford had finally ceased production of them in favor of newer, flashier mass-produced vehicles of the American dream). His father had worked on his beloved toy whenever time allowed, trying to keep it running for those occasional Sunday joy rides with the children of his first marriage. A practiced nostalgist himself, he had decided to use his father's birthday this year (this year of the stroke and the wheelchair and the ever-worsening cough of emphysema) to revive these gauzy memories. He contacted a local classic car collectors' club to see if any Model T enthusiasts would consent to give an original but unofficial member of their charter a birthday ride back up memory lane. His query was answered promptly by a call from Mr. Cy Vogel, who happily agreed to drive over from Painesville to their Maple Street home in Perry, no more than a 15-minute jaunt in a modern road-eating sedan but nearly an hour's trek in the wheezing jalopy, to help deliver the present. (Cy had done similar favors before, and he always enjoyed the opportunity to preach to the converted about the wonders of his still-bucking steed.)

Please imagine the music starting up now, the organist in black tails adding little flourishes as he accompanies the authentically grayscale two-reeler playing out on the screen above. Imagine, in the utility room that gave onto the kitchen, a series of close-ups: old woolen waistcoat wrapped around hunched shoulders, gloves being pulled onto ecchymotic hands, another scarf being wrapped around an age-wrinkled neck, boots being pulled on before the feet are resettled onto the wheelchair supports, and a ski cap pulled down onto a bald head (though with some white fringe ringed above the ears and a few last wisps waving from the forehead). Cut to the jalopy outside, its driver honking the bicycle horn attached apocryphally to the windshield as he waves cheerily to the house and the bustle in the utility room. Cut again to the grownup son, smiling as he dons a thick, furry, pleated winter hat of the Russian astrakhan genre, pulling it down in back to cover his ears, and then comically reaches for the biggest umbrella in the stand (to ward off, as much as possible, the thickening snow from the unsheltered mother-in-law's seat in back). The next shot shows his mother standing at the screen door as her husband is lifted into the passenger side of the cab, his feet being placed on the floorboard, his legs and chest covered with a thick woolen blanket done in Tartan pattern, his grin as he looks down the hood of this mythical chariot crooked but real.

The organist picks up the tempo a bit for a cut to a long shot from the north, up Maple Street a little way, where you can see the contraption turn right and head toward Perry Township proper. The camera initially holds still as the Model T rocks and snorts and gathers a bit of speed, the driver gesticulating and already deep into his docent routine, pointing up at the canopy, down to the three pedals that he works awkwardly, ahead toward the laboring engine block, preaching to a single, helplessly happy chorister about the categorical superiority of a dying past. The camera pans left with the Silver-less carriage's labored passing, and you can see the son in the back, his umbrella protruding comically from all the bundling.

A brief montage sequence will now show the one-vehicle parade passing by city hall, the library, and even old Perry High. A more eager nostalgist of a director might even cut inside the halls for a shot of the fading, yellowed snapshot, in a trophy case just outside the gym, of the future umbrella-toting preacher as a very skinny, very young man, grinning in his track suit as he holds up several ribbons. If the director and the camera operator dolly in far enough on this picture of apparent triumph, viewers might even notice a swollen lower lip and a bruise-darkened left eye and wonder. What could have caused this happy, decorated sprinter to get into a fight on the eve of his triumph and leave him so marked? What kind of insult had been delivered to the masked ranger's acolyte to prompt him to fisticuffs? But before such speculations will end, this public image of the mythologized past will, of course, dissolve into the present-past version, ribbonless under the umbrella and fur hat, his eyes surprisingly hard as he ponders the figure of his father in front of him.

A sterner sort of impresario might delay the end of the tiny procession by diverting it past the town's oldest graveyard, where the prize passenger would soon be laid in rest, arresting the camera's gaze at the arched cemetery gates, and letting the wheezing jalopy pass and escape the frame. The camera would move in closer to emphasize the dark stones etched with names and dates, most of them too obscure in the swirling snow to make out, their presence suggested but not individualized, until it focuses on one that looks newer than the others around it, one with a single syllable of a last name, one that had been visited surreptitiously in recent months by an old woman with a different last name, an old woman whose curls had once been black but whose remaining hair was perhaps even whiter than the snow that was falling on the dead and the quick alike all around the little town.

The final sequence of the film will begin (as the organist subtly slows the tempo) with an exterior shot of the family home before cutting to a three-quarter eye-level

124

perspective (the "American shot") on his mother standing in the living room, looking out the picture window as the snow falls more thickly, the wind whipping it into a cinegenic frenzy that Murnau might have been tempted to use in the opening scene for his aging, heavyset, nameless hotel doorman. Will viewers now know that she's thinking of a third man, much taller than her husband, as tall as her son, in fact, a man she has mythologized in a different way, a man who effectively brought her husband and son together before the former banished him from her life forever? Maybe the sequence will even dissolve from the hard look in the son's eyes as he sits behind his father under the umbrella to the equally hard look in hers standing at the window, and maybe, just maybe, the viewer will catch a hint of all the things that, it was long ago decided, had to be left unsaid.

Cut back to the driver, looking anxiously up at the gathering storm and then smiling encouragingly at his shivering passenger. It's time to wind the parade down, time to make his way back home to Painesville. But when the camera pans to his tight-lipped passenger, the crooked grin is gone and the pleading eyes are unmistakable, pleading a reprieve, pleading a little more time on this unexpected flight of freedom for the aged, stricken birthday boy.

The feeder reel in front will be almost empty now, only a few short revolutions left, but the take-up reel will be almost full, winding slowly with the burden of all those images. We will not again focus on the faithful white-haired woman in the home, peering out the window as the delegation rumbles into sight. Instead, she will just appear, unobtrusively, in the deep background of the shot, a figure glimpsed in passing by eagle-eyed viewers only, as the camera pans right to catch the wain as it continues south, past the house. And then, eventually, the horizontal sweep of the camera will be arrested in favor of a slow tilt upward that will, for a little while longer, manage to keep the vehicle in frame as it takes the hill, backfiring once or twice before disappearing altogether into the billowing clouds of snow.

Rafael Zepeda

The Professionals

They were living in London then, "by hook or by crook," as they say, when they saw *The Professionals,* at a posh theatre in Leicester Square, one of the big theatres that served hard drinks and beer and wine in its red-velvet-curtained lobby. They were drinking pints of Watney's. Gordon, a Canadian friend from Montreal, and West often scraped together a couple of pounds and went to see American movies, especially Westerns. It made them both feel like they were cowboys from the past for two hours or so. North Americans. As if they were home for a few minutes. It was The Sixties and they'd both been living in Europe for a couple of years. Back then, when someone was away from the States or Canada—perhaps when everyone was away from their so called "home"—no matter how fucked up home was—Stupid War or no Stupid War—they started to miss things at about three months, then six months, then they exponentially missed things very badly in a year. Those time intervals were like kilometer posts on the side of the road as one drove toward their destination. After that, the longer a person was away, the further apart those kilometer posts got, since the people and places of home were so very far away, that place now foreign to them, because of things changing— new buildings, new situations, new people, new governments. Now, more than fifty years later, the internet and the cell phone had changed this, West knew. Parents and their children, and friends, were now in contact with each other almost all of the time now, not lost in a foreign country where it cost too much for a phone call home, West thought, if there was even a telephone there to call someone, where no one knows you, or speaks your language. When West was away for two years, one time, he had spoken to his parents on the phone only twice. That was enough back then, West thought. Or so it had seemed.

Lee Marvin, and Burt Lancaster, and Robert Ryan, and Woody Strode, and Jack Palance are in *The Professionals,* all of them having been great actors in many great films, cowboy films or otherwise. Marvin is the leader, a kind of sergeant; Lancaster knows explosives; Ryan is a lover of horses and a wrangler; Strode is an expert with the long bow; Jack Palance is a Mexican- revolutionary leader.

Again, Gordon and West were in London during The Sixties. A lot was going on in London then, West thought. Everyone has heard about that time. Gordon and West were both involved in all that people had heard about London at that time. People then were all looking for something, and most of them had no idea what that thing that they were looking for was.

In one scene in the film Marvin, Lancaster, Ryan and Strode are in a narrow canyon shooting their Winchesters at Jack Palance, the Mexican-revolutionary-leader Jesus Raza. And Raza and his followers are shooting back at them. There is a woman there, Rosa, who is also a revolutionary, and a few of Raza's men are behind him in the rocks. Everyone is hiding behind some rocks in the canyon, and between shots Raza and Lancaster and Rosa are shouting in a friendly way to each other. They're old friends, having fought together in The Mexican Revolution in the past. Then Rosa comes charging from behind the rocks toward Lancaster, and he shoots her, dead. Jesus Raza watches her die, unable to help her; he is just trying to get his girlfriend, the beautiful Claudia Cardinale, back from the four Americans. They've snatched her from his camp for a rich gringo, her husband, risking their lives, this time, for money, not for the good of the people, as the four did in the past, Will and Gordon realize. They're discussing the separate roads that they've traveled since the old days, talking about risking their lives, for "a cause" instead of money. Then Raza shouts down the canyon to Lancaster:

"Without a cause we are nothing...

We stay because we believe…
We leave because we are disillusioned…
We come back because we are lost…
We die because are committed…"

Burt Lancaster is thinking about the time he spent fighting for The Revolution, about the revolutionary woman, Rosa, that he has just shot and killed, who was once his lover. There is quiet there in the canyon. Then horses are galloping through the canyon somewhere behind Lancaster. Lancaster has planted dynamite in the rocks above the canyon, but now he is remembering when he was young, when Rosa was his lover and the lover of many other revolutionaries, and how she was a part of their cause, as he was. He is listening to the galloping of the horses as it grows faint. Then he touches the fuse with his lit cigar and in a few moments the dynamite explodes, and huge rocks fall and tumble down to the canyon floor, stopping Raza's progress, if only for a while. We were young, Lancaster thinks, and it was a cause worth risking our lives for…

An hour later, at the train tracks, up North and across the border in the states, the four professionals meet the old gringo, who has their cash waiting for them. Claudia is sitting in a wagon, the reins in her hands. Two of the old gringo's men stand behind him, their rifles ready. Claudia sits in the wagon and doesn't move. Her tan shirt is unbuttoned to just below her breasts, the shirt sweaty and dirt stained. Her face glistens in the sun and her nostrils are flared. She stares at her husband, the old gringo, with her round, brown eyes. He holds the promised money in his right hand, a big pile of bills. Then Jesus Raza, who we now see has been lying in the back of the wagon, sits up. He is wounded and he is bleeding. The old gringo tells his men, "Shoot him! Kill him!" His two men just stand there, so he grabs one of their rifles. Marvin steps in front of him." You haven't earned the right to kill him," Marvin says. And Claudia says, "Jesus and I have been lovers since we were children. You knew this when I was forced to marry you. I won't go back to you. My parents made me marry you, all because of your money. But I don't care about your money. And I don't care about you." She pulls back the reins with her right hand, and the horses turn the wagon around, and she rolls South toward Mexico again. "You keep your money," Marvin says. "It looks as if your wife is gone again. This time for good." The old gringo says, "You dirty bastards." And Marvin says, "Perhaps we are, but you, sir, are a self-made man."

The four professionals mount up, pull back on their reins and turn and head South again, as well. Perhaps they are going back to join The Revolution, once again. Perhaps. Gordon and West thought then about causes as they left the posh theatre and walked through the red-velvet-covered lobby. Then they stood in The Chelsea Potter, their pub, and drank Watney's bitter. Some of their friends were fighting a war that they didn't understand and didn't want to fight. Their cause, Wes and Gordon thought, was to not join that *cause* that the generals had constructed in a lie that was as huge as the Gobi Desert over many years, they realized that most causes lost their glimmer when they went on and on, without solutions. But they continued to look for another cause, nevertheless. They asked their friends and those people that they met, "Do you know of a cause worth following? Do you have a cause? Is that thing worth fighting for?"

(Author's Note: West's friend, Paul, a very good painter, called one Tuesday evening and said that he had just seen *The Professionals* again on television that morning. He reminded West what Jesus Raza had said to Burt Lancaster in the canyon. So when he hung up the phone West recalled this day long ago with his friend, Gordon, and then its echoes over the years.)

129

Nonfiction

Dibakar Barua

Satyajit Ray and the Bengali Cinema
Satyajit Ray & Rabindranath Tagore

Two great artists India has brought forth in the 20th century, both from the eastern province of Bengal, are poet, novelist, and composer Rabindranath Tagore and filmmaker Satyajit Ray. Tagore has the unique distinction of writing songs that would become the national anthems of two modern nations, India and Bangladesh, and one cannot begin to assess modern Bengali cultural and literary identity without reckoning with the pervasive influence of his immense oeuvre—poetry, fiction, songs, and essays—on the Bengali consciousness. Satyajit Ray himself was a product of this Rabindric Bengali culture. The family history of the two men is intertwined. Ray's grandfather—writer, philosopher, and publisher Upendrakishore Ray—was a friend of Rabindranath Tagore, and it is at Tagore's university (Visva Bharati) that Satyajit received his first training in Indian art that would shape his early career as a graphic design artist and also leave a distinctive mark on his later film art. Ray will go on to make a landmark documentary on the life of Rabindranath and three of his major films would be based on the poet's short stories and novels.

A Political Digression

What was the province of Bengal in British India was split into two different and ideologically opposed territories with the partition of India in 1947: West Bengal, a state in the Hindu majority India, and East Bengal a province of the Muslim majority Pakistan. I was born in East Bengal (renamed East Pakistan in 1955) and grew up in a political and cultural climate where all things Indian—including Tagore's writings and Ray's films—were considered by the

131

ruling elite as antithetical to the national interest of promoting an Islamic identity.

In the 1950s & 60s, East Pakistan labored against and resisted a concerted campaign of political and cultural hegemony by West Pakistan. The West Pakistani elite that dominated the newly formed country's government had declared Urdu to be the national language of the new nation, thus relegating Bengali, the language of the nation's non-contiguous province that was the home of its numerically largest ethnic group, to a secondary status as either a national language or as a medium of instruction. This politically purblind attempt at domination would escalate into two decades of political feud between the Pakistani ruling class aided by the military and the people of East Bengal, culminating into the paroxysmal emergence of Bangladesh as a new South Asian nation in 1971 after a genocidal civil war.

From its very inception, Jinnah's Pakistan valorized religion over all other identities — cultural, linguistic, ethnic, tribal — that marked the subcontinent's incredible diversity throughout the centuries. After the partition of 1947, India was able, despite all its failures and periodic flare ups, to construct a secular democratic character that remained relatively stable until recently under the Modi regime. Pakistan, on the other hand, never enjoyed even a semblance of a secular democracy, weathering a series of violent upheavals, alternating between civilian rule and military juntas, in every decade of its existence. Religion cannot cement the fissures that crackle when democratic values are subjugated to competing parochial interests.

After 24 years of an uneasy and rocky political union based on religion, Bangladesh broke away from Pakistan because its cultural and geographical identity proved to be stronger than the religious one. The first rupture between the two wings of Pakistan occurred over the question of language. The greatest national commemoration and festival in Bangladesh is not its Independence Day, but *Shahid Dibash*, or Martyr's Day, aka *Bhasha Dibash* or language day, which falls on 21st February. On that day in 1952, four students, peacefully protesting the imposition of Urdu as East Bengal's national language, lost their lives to police gunfire. Since then, *Amar Ekushey*, the immortal 21st, became the rallying cry of the Bengali population against political and cultural subjugation by the Pakistani elite.

Ray's Absence in East Bengal

I make this political digression to point out that though Satyajit Ray was the greatest Bengali filmmaker of his time and remains so today, Bengalis living in East Pakistan, comprising the majority of all Bengalis, had no access to his cinema. Pakistan and India had fought two wars between 1947 and 1965 over the disputed territory of Kashmir and eyed each other as enemies bereft of diplomatic relations. Culturally, the Pakistani rulers were suspicious of all Bengali cultural expressions—especially poetry and songs they considered "Hindu" rather than Bengali. The "Bhasha Dibash" celebrants would sing songs by Rabindranath Tagore, so the Pakistani dictator Ayub Khan imposed a ban on Tagore songs in 1965. There was also an attempt to Islamize Bengali, and I recall reading poems in school textbooks, where Arabic, Urdu, or Persian words would be substituted for more Sanskrit derived Bengali words, with a total bowdlerizing disregard for the original content.

By some fluke, though, a Ray film, *Mahanagar* (1963), was shown in Dhaka in the late 1960s. I was attending college in the port city Chittagong then, and only heard of the long lines that formed in front of the cinema hall, and that hundreds, if not thousands, had to be turned away. For my own first Ray film, I had to wait until March 1972, just a few months after the liberation of Bangladesh.

As a student at Dhaka University, I had joined a Film Society, probably the very first one In Bangladesh, which, like the Calcutta Film Society founded by Satyajit Ray, arranged for international films to be screened for its membership. These films were screened in various venues,

133

sometimes in movie halls but mostly in performing art centers where screens would be set up and projectors were brought in. One could hear the whirring of the 16mm movie reels and see a beam of light overhead. Before a film was screened, a card would be dropped in my room noting the film to be screened, the time, and the venue. However, this one time, the card had no film title, simply a note that a special film would be screened. I went out of my room to catch the courier and asked him, "What is it—French, Italian?" He hushed me with a raised forefinger to his lips and whispered, "Just come to the screening."

The film was *Charulata* (1964), which Ray himself considered to be his favorite film. Remembering the stampede for *Mahanagar* a few years ago, I understood the need for the courier's secrecy and counted my blessings for this unexpected opportunity to see my very first Satyajit Ray film, at age 21, in an intimate setting. Alas, the inexperience of the projector operator created moments of great confusion because after the first reel, he started showing the third, skipping the second one by mistake. Jarred by discontinuity, the audience howled; the screening was interrupted for about twenty minutes, so the error could be rectified.

Ray's Artistry

Charulata, of course, was nothing like what I had seen before of Indian cinema. Shunning all the conventions of a popular Bollywood production—artificial sets, fantastic plots, and elaborate song-dance-fight routines—Ray began the film with a muted musical score and a slow opening sequence where nothing happens for eight minutes except for a lonely housewife doing embroidery, humming a song, listlessly opening a book, pacing, and looking out of the windows of a prosperous Victorian home at street peddlers and random walkers through her opera glasses. An elegant mood of loneliness, boredom, melancholy, and longing is firmly established. This was cinema of the director as the auteur,

134

shaping each aspect of the film including lighting, set design, musical score, and screenplay. The film develops its gorgeously slow movement to include a breathtaking montage of the main character swinging in her garden while recollecting childhood memories, to the devastating emotional climax of its ending where an irreparable emotional gulf between husband and wife is revealed.

Based on Tagore's novella *Nashtanir* (*Broken Nest*), *Charulata* is a compact emotional drama commonly speculated to have been based on some autobiographical elements in Tagore's life involving an emotional triangle between a young Tagore, his elder brother, twelve years his senior, and his sister-in-law Kadambari Devi, who was just a couple of years older than Tagore. In real life that triangle ended in tragedy because Kadambari Devi committed suicide a few months after Tagore's hastily arranged marriage. Tagore's novella eschews tragedy but explores the emotional anguish that results from the stultifying gender roles of the 19th century. Ray makes good use of his sources in Tagore's writings, using not only the story but a few songs too and creating a meticulous period setting to capture a prosperous home in 1880s Calcutta; he also reconceives the story with an original screenplay that gives the wife a vibrant agency.

Satyajit Ray is one of the best screenplay writers of all time. He wrote the screenplays for each of his three dozen feature films, and being the graphic artist he was, he also illustrated them copiously with image sequences for the storyboard. Furthermore, after directing his first six films, Ray also took on the task of creating musical scores for his films. He employed the best musicians and composers he could find but was ultimately unhappy with their work. When Ray came to New York, in 1981, for a retrospective of his films in the Little Carnegie Theater, I had an opportunity to ask him about his decision to compose his own scores. His answer was that while he felt a rapport with Ravi Shankar for the Apu trilogy films, the compositions by others—Vilayat Khan and Ali Akbar Khan—did not fully comport with his vision for the theme and mood of his films. Vilayat Khan had composed what most would consider a gorgeous score for *The Music Room* (1958). But for Ray, it missed the point: "Vilayat Khan … didn't see the point of feudalism dying out… he composed the most wonderful noble themes for the film…. I would have given it an ironic edge to it, even from the beginning, suggesting the doom that was coming. But for him it was all sweetness and greatness." [1]

Direction, screenplay, music, light, sound, camera, location scouting, discovering and training actors, and building an ensemble he could rely upon—Ray took on the mantle of an auteur at the inception of his filmmaking career. As a young movie buff, while working as an art director at a British ad agency, he had founded the Calcutta Film Society in 1947, just after India's independence. Ray also reminisces how, during his employment related trip to London, he had seen films of the Italian neorealist directors. After watching *The Bicycle Thief* by De Sica, he had an epiphany—that he could also make a film without relying on studios or professional actors—just getting a camera, having a good script, and having a keen grasp of human emotions was enough. On his way back from London, during his passage on a ship, he wrote the first draft of his first screenplay based on the novel *Pather Panchali* by Bibhutibhusan Bandopadhyay. In 1950, Jean Renoir came to Calcutta to shoot his film *The River*. Ray, who had not seen Renoir's great French films at that time, worked with Renoir on scouting locations and was encouraged by Renoir to make his script into a film.

Anyone who has read the two novels by Bibhutibhusan Bandopadhyay—*Pather Panchali* and *Aparajito*—on which the celebrated Apu Trilogy is based (*Pather Panchali* (1955), *Aparajito* (1956), *Apur Songsar* (1959))—will be struck by Ray's radical reconception of literary material for the creation of film art of the highest order. It is worth repeating what an undisputed master of cinema, Akira Kurosawa, had said about Ray's art after watching the Apu Trilogy and other Ray films:

Not to have seen the cinema of Ray means existing in the world without seeing the sun or the moon. I can never forget the excitement in my mind after seeing it (*Pather Panchali*). It is the kind of cinema that flows with the serenity and nobility of a big river. People are born, live out their lives, and then accept their deaths. Without the least effort and without any sudden jerks, Ray paints his picture, but its effect on the audience is to stir up deep passions. How does he achieve this? There is nothing irrelevant or haphazard in his cinematographic technique. In that lies the secret of its excellence. [2]

The two novels on which the trilogy is based are distinguished works of Bengali literature. However, while *Pather Panchali*, the novel, is a memorable chronicle of a rural family and community in British Bengal, *Aparajito*, the sequel, continues the classic bildungsroman focused on Apu, the young boy of the first novel, and traces his development into adolescence and adulthood. In writing these two novels, Bandopadhyay blends realism with lyrical evocations of landscape and character that also conveys a larger cosmic vision of life—through all its permutations of birth, romance, celebrations, rituals, suffering, and death—as an eternal and ultimately joyful recurrence, in the vein of what Huxley calls a perennial philosophy.

What Ray does with this evocative but amorphous literary material is nothing short of a miracle. He had no intention of making the second film until he saw the warm reception his first film received, and after the second film went on to receive even greater acclaim than the first—winning the golden lion at Venice—Ray thought he was done with the Bandopadhyay's novels; he went on to film another remarkable film—*The Music Room*—before returning to the story of Apu in 1959. Yet, taken together, the trilogy presents a great cinematic triumph held together by character, theme, and narrative mastery.

In writing about Ray's art, I am acutely aware that many writers and critics, with more expertise on Ray and cinema, have written on the subject. Two motifs stand out from the available evaluation—such as by Pauline Kael and Robin Wood: that the apparent simplicity of Ray's work is the product of a mature and scholarly artist who deftly incorporated various techniques he admired in Jean Renoir, Vittorio De Sica, and many other film artists; that there is Mozartian aspect of balance and counterpoint in his major films that create both emotional complexity and aesthetic delight. [3] To this I will add a third, more literary perspective—his broad range and compassionate humanity that tempts one to posit an analogy with Shakespeare. Ray began by depicting rural Bengal in British India in the Apu Trilogy and went on to explore, quite masterfully, a wide variety of subjects in his oeuvre of 39 films—feudal decadence, social corruption, postcolonial urban unrest, famine, fantasy and fairy tale, Tagore, Ibsen, documentaries, short films, and more. It is instructive also to compare Ray's oeuvre with that of two other celebrated Bengali filmmakers of his generation—Ritwik Ghatak and Mrinal Sen. All three of them are considered pioneers of new wave cinema in India. The one dominant theme in Ghatak's major films (for example, *Meghe Dhaka Tara* and *Subarnarekha*) is the partition of India in 1947, specifically the partition of Bengal and the tragedy and struggles that followed due to mass migration of displaced people. In the films of Mrinal Sen, a self-described "private Marxist," the theme is both the oppression of poor people by the rich and powerful and the inner and outer corruption that engulfs and ruins innocence. This specialized focus in the films of Ghatak and Sen tends to take on an ideological orientation and a didactic bent that is completely absent in Ray. Watching a film by Ritwik Ghatak or Mrinal Sen, and I know this is a risky generalization, I am often aware that I am watching a constructed story with a message. Watching Ray, for the most part, I am absorbed in the full presence of life presented in multiple layers of significance which only grows in richness and resonance with repeated viewing. I am reminded of what Virginia Woolf says, in *A Room of One's Own*, about the difference between art with an agenda or gripes, as in the novels of Galsworthy, Kipling, or even Charlotte Bronte, and art that transcends all personal impediments with an incandescent, androgynous mind—as in Shakespeare. Ray's films are irresistible because, to quote W. B. Yeats, "Only that which does not teach, which does not persuade, which does not cry out, which does not condescend, which does not explain, is irresistible." [(4)]

Kurosawa's comments on *Pather Panchali* captures something ineffable and yet essential in understanding and appreciating Ray's art. The first time I saw this film, the work of a mostly amateur group of actors, director, cameraman, editor, art director, and even composer (this was Ravi Shankar's first film score), each sequence appeared to me as a revelation, life captured in all its beauty, pathos, harshness, and complexity—yes, this truly is what life in the village was like for people of genteel poverty, people I have known so closely in my own family. It was a shock of deep recognition—these people, images, sights, sounds, gestures, events are so true to my being, in some genetic or cultural inheritance that waited for articulation in great art. Sounds and images kept haunting me for days, months, and years—a smoke-belching train bisecting a vast rice field, its hiss and clangor obliterating the innocence of children playing among the downy *kash* grass; old dying auntie dozing by a bamboo grove, falling headfirst with a thud onto the hard ground when nudged by the curious children; water flies skittering on a shimmering pond, and lily pads lifting in the wind before an ecstatic rainstorm drenches the parched country; a Ganesh-idol shaken by the screeching storm, as a frantic mother tries to sooth her dying girl while her brother innocently sleeps; a mother's wail of grief captured by the piercing melody of a tar Sanai; and after the girl's death, Apu finding the stolen bead-necklace she guiltily hid, and the quietly grieving boy throwing it into a pond where it plops momentarily to be covered slowly by the pond scum. Pauline Kael says about a vastly different film Ray made fifteen years later (*Days & Nights in the Forest*, 1970), "Satyajit Ray's films can give rise to a more complex feeling of happiness…than the work of any other director." This happiness—so poetically resonant in *Pather Panchali*, and becoming more musical, contrapuntal, and dramatic in his diverse work of a breathtaking range—lies in the aesthetic presentation of incidents and images that dovetail the physical and the spiritual, the sociohistorical and the psychological and hold up an exquisite mirror. This is not to say there is no lapse of energy in the Ray films. There definitely is, especially some of his last films that he made in failing health, but for the most part, Satyajit Ray is a master filmmaker who has presented the world with at least a score of unforgettable masterpieces of cinema. The only reason he is not a more well-known name globally—like Fellini or Kurosawa—is that his films are all about Bengal, a place of little geopolitical importance and uses a language that even the vast majority of Indians do not speak or feel the need to learn.

Satyajit Ray in Bangladesh

Unlike Ritwik Ghatak, whose main theme is the partition of Bengal that eventually led to a massive displacement of people, Ray never evinced a personal and political attachment to the idea of a Bengali identity. He did collaborate with a Bangladeshi actor in his 1975 film *Ashani Sanket* (*Distant Thunder*), and it is said that he wanted to make a film about the Bangladesh liberation movement but abandoned the idea because he felt temperamentally unsuited for films with overtly political content. On February 21, 1972, just two months after the liberation of Bangladesh, on the occasion of the very first Shahid Dibash of independent Bangladesh, a student union arranged a massive public celebration at Paltan Maidan, a huge empty space in a corner of Dhaka used for political gatherings. Satyajit Ray was the chief guest on this occasion, and he delivered a memorable speech in Bengali. Below is a translation with a few minor deletions:

I have been hearing about February 21, "Shaheed Dibosh" for a long time. But if I had not come here and seen it for myself, I couldn't have understood how much you love

140

the Bangla language. I realized how much you respect those who laid down their lives to save Bangla when it faced great danger.

We who live in West Bengal also love the Bangla language. It's true that the culture of West Bengal has a mixed form as it has been influenced by a number of other cultures. We haven't been able to get rid of the English influence as yet. Perhaps one of the reasons for this is that West Bengal is just one province of India. But that doesn't mean that we don't love Bangla. Bangla literature and songs, Bangla films, theatre—all these are still alive in West Bengal. We still love Rabindranath, Nazrul, Bankim, and Sarat.

Personally, I have been making Bangla films for twenty years now. During this time, I got many requests from many places to leave Bangla and make films in other languages in other countries. But I have rejected those offers over and over again. I know that the language which runs in my blood is the Bangla language. I know that if I leave this language and try to do something in any other, then I will have no ground under my feet; I will not find any base as an artist; I will lose all my spirit and energy.

I have heard from my childhood that East Bengal is my home. Perhaps some of you have heard about my grandfather, Upendra Kishore Ray. I did not have the good fortune of meeting him, but I read his children's story books…and loved them. Songs written by him gave me a taste of eastern Bangla folk songs. I had never been to this country, never been to my home, and never been here permanently: but whenever I heard these songs and fairy tales, I felt a deep connection with this country. I came to Dhaka once when I was five or six years old. I stayed here for only 2-3 days… I remember travelling on a steamer through the Padma. As I awoke early in the morning, my Ma pointed out the sun rising over the Padma. She also showed me how the two colors of Padma and Jamuna were different and could be seen easily when they mingled. From then on, I had thought many times that it would be great to visit my home. But that hope kept receding particularly after the partition.

Suddenly, the wheels of history seemed to turn, the door of my home opened and today, on the "Shaheed Dibash," standing in front of you all, my dream is being partly fulfilled. I have come here leaving many important things. That's why I cannot stay for long. But I still hope to come back here in the future. I will observe this country closely. I want to meet the people not in a public meeting but face-to-face...

I already know that you know about my work and want to know more. A few years ago, my film *Mahanagar* was shown here. The interest of the people, their curiosity, and the result of these—when I first heard, I did not believe them. But then, many known and unknown friends wrote to me, sent me paper-cuttings about the incidents to make me believe them. Then, I believed them and was stunned by all those happenings. I couldn't imagine that this could happen. For an artist, a greater honor or a greater pride cannot be imagined.

In the last twenty years, I have been honored by many people in many countries. But today, standing in the holy hour of Shaheed Dibosh, I can confidently say that the respect and honor given to me today, has surpassed all the others of the past. I have never received a greater honor and I don't think that I will ever receive any—Joy Bangla! (Victory to Bengal) [5]

Notes

[1] *Satyajit Ray: An Anthology of Statements on Ray and by Ray.* Ed. Chidananda Dasgupta. Directorate of Film Festivals, New Delhi. 1981. Page 38.

[2] "Akira Kurosawa said Watching a Satyajit Ray Film Is Like 'Seeing the Sun or Moon'" https://www.indiewire.com/2015/05/akira-kurosawa-said-watching-a-satyajit-ray-film-is-like-seeing-the-sun-or-moon-187504/

[3] *Satyajit Ray: An Anthology of Statements on Ray and by Ray.* Ed. Chidananda Dasgupta. Directorate of Film Festivals, New Delhi. 1981. Page 85.

[4] https://minimalistquotes.com/william-butler-yeats-quote-133470/

[5] Tabibul Islam (Babu), "Satyajit Roy's Memorable Speech at Dhaka." https://www.thedailystar.net/supplements/amar-ekushey-2016/satyajit-roys-memorable-speech-dhaka-575185

The Other Side of the Whirlwind

Mr. Welles, My Father, and the Dark Art of Film

For a time in my twenties I got by doing grunt work on a string of ultra-low-budget movies. Low as in dogs, rubbish, bottom-line write-offs shot fast and dirty at so many LA rent-a-locations. An abandoned warehouse downtown. A smoky airport strip club. Some rich guy's glassed-in pile up in the hills.

Up till then my days had felt mostly lost and aimless, like being stuck in a life not quite your own. The question plaguing me was, what to do with a BA in English after all the other gigs I was cycling through: singing busboy, taxicab hack, housepainter, ditchdigger, fry cook. A writer, I'd heard, needed experiences to write about so I was trying to get some—and now?

My friend Greg McCarty, sharper than I was, had studied not literature but film at UCLA, and on to a directing fellowship at the American Film Institute. While I was emptying ashtrays or scraping paint Greg was now crewing on the thesis film of future Oscar nominee Gill Dennis, interning on the Texas set of *The Getaway* under the notorious Sam Peckinpah.

But we were friends, Greg and me, so whenever he thought we could swing it I'd slip in the back way to the AFI's Greystone Mansion for special screenings, shop talks by visiting industry notables, etc. Robert Towne, for example, still coming to grips with the changes Roman Polanski had made to Towne's original *Chinatown* script, changes that transformed a propulsive neo-noir murder mystery into the sublimest of tragedies as our rogue detective's struggle to protect his desperate client-lover ends with a bullet through her skull and evil triumphant in the rapacious figure of her father; not to mention that unforgettable curtain line about forgetting it. [1]

We felt like spies stealing secrets, like we'd be breaking the bank now, any day. Plus, nobody ever kicked me out.

At AFI Greg met the lovely, level-headed Marti Bercaw, an art-directing Fellow from Hamilton, Ohio. Soon enough they had moved in together and then they had graduated, and Marti the only one among us going on to do what she had been schooled to do through the seesaw uncertainties of the coming years.

Exhilarating, that seesaw? In spades, at least the upside. How else to describe all those nights the three of us spent in movie-lover's bliss at the fabulous Fox Venice, the city's preeminent revival house. At ninety-nine cents a ticket for an adroitly curated double feature that changed five times a week, what more could a striving scribbler hope for?

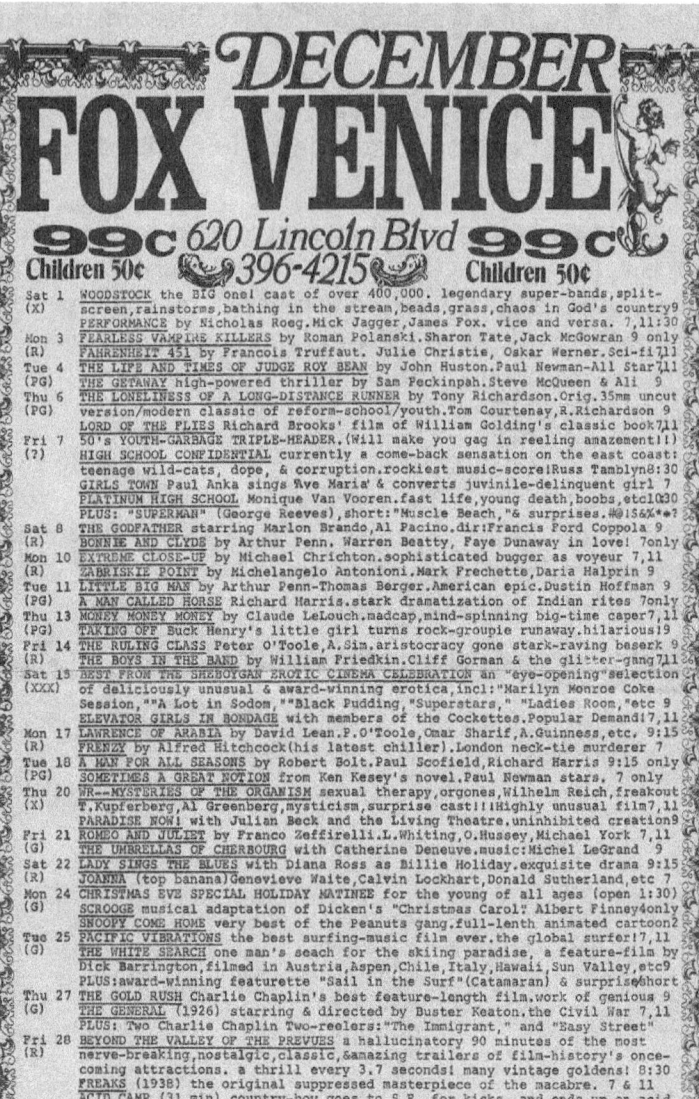

DECEMBER
FOX VENICE

99¢ 620 Lincoln Blvd **99¢**
Children 50¢ 396-4215 Children 50¢

Sat 1
(X) WOODSTOCK the BIG one! cast of over 400,000. legendary super-bands,split-
screen,rainstorms,bathing in the stream,beads,grass,chaos in God's country9
PERFORMANCE by Nicholas Roeg.Mick Jagger,James Fox. vice and versa. 7,11:30

Mon 3
(R) FEARLESS VAMPIRE KILLERS by Roman Polanski.Sharon Tate,Jack McGowran 9 only
FAHRENHEIT 451 by Francois Truffaut. Julie Christie, Oskar Werner.Sci-fi 7,11

Tue 4
(PG) THE LIFE AND TIMES OF JUDGE ROY BEAN by John Huston.Paul Newman-All Star 7,11
THE GETAWAY high-powered thriller by Sam Peckinpah.Steve McQueen & Ali 9

Thu 6
(PG) THE LONELINESS OF A LONG-DISTANCE RUNNER by Tony Richardson.Orig.35mm uncut
version/modern classic of reform-school/youth.Tom Courtenay,R.Richardson 9
LORD OF THE FLIES Richard Brooks' film of William Golding's classic book 7,11

Fri 7
(?) 50's YOUTH-GARBAGE TRIPLE-HEADER.(Will make you gag in reeling amazement!!)
HIGH SCHOOL CONFIDENTIAL currently a come-back sensation on the east coast!
teenage wild-cats, dope, & corruption.rockiest music-score!Russ Tamblyn8:30
GIRLS TOWN Paul Anka sings Ave Maria' & converts juvinile-delinquent girl 7
PLATINUM HIGH SCHOOL Monique Van Vooren.fast life,young death,boobs,etc10:30
PLUS: "SUPERMAN" (George Reeves),short:"Muscle Beach,"& surprises.#@!S&%*•?

Sat 8
(R) THE GODFATHER starring Marlon Brando,Al Pacino.dir:Francis Ford Coppola 9

Mon 10
(R) BONNIE AND CLYDE by Arthur Penn. Warren Beatty, Faye Dunaway in love! 7only
EXTREME CLOSE-UP by Michael Chrichton.sophisticated bugger as voyeur 7,11

Tue 11
(PG) ZABRISKIE POINT by Michelangelo Antonioni.Mark Frechette,Daria Halprin 9
LITTLE BIG MAN by Arthur Penn-Thomas Berger.American epic.Dustin Hoffman 9

Thu 13
(PG) A MAN CALLED HORSE Richard Harris.stark dramatization of Indian rites 7only
MONEY MONEY MONEY by Claude LeLouch.madcap,mind-spinning big-time caper7,11

Fri 14
(R) TAKING OFF Buck Henry's little girl turns rock-groupie runaway.hilarious!9
THE RULING CLASS Peter O'Toole,A.Sim.aristocracy gone stark-raving beserk 9

Sat 15
(XXX) THE BOYS IN THE BAND by William Friedkin.Cliff Gorman & the glitter-gang 7,11
BEST FROM THE SHEBOYGAN EROTIC CINEMA CELEBRATION an "eye-opening"selection
of deliciously unusual & award-winning erotica,incl:"Marilyn Monroe Coke
Session,""A Lot in Sodom,""Black Pudding,"Superstars," "Ladies Room,"etc 9
ELEVATOR GIRLS IN BONDAGE with members of the Cockettes.Popular Demand!7,11

Mon 17
(R) LAWRENCE OF ARABIA by David Lean.P.O'Toole,Omar Sharif,A.Guinness,etc. 9:15
FRENZY by Alfred Hitchcock(his latest chiller).London neck-tie murderer 7

Tue 18
(PG) A MAN FOR ALL SEASONS by Robert Bolt.Paul Scofield,Richard Harris 9:15 only
SOMETIMES A GREAT NOTION from Ken Kesey's novel.Paul Newman stars. 7 only

Thu 20
(X) WR--MYSTERIES OF THE ORGANISM sexual therapy,orgones,Wilhelm Reich,freakout
T.Kupferberg,Al Greenberg,mysticism,surprise cast!!!Highly unusual film7,11
PARADISE NOW! with Julian Beck and the Living Theatre.uninhibited creation9

Fri 21
(G) ROMEO AND JULIET by Franco Zeffirelli.L.Whiting,O.Hussey,Michael York 7,11
THE UMBRELLAS OF CHERBOURG with Catherine Deneuve.music:Michel LeGrand 9

Sat 22
(R) LADY SINGS THE BLUES with Diana Ross as Billie Holiday.exquisite drama 9:15
JOANNA (top banana)Genevieve Waite,Calvin Lockhart,Donald Sutherland,etc 7

Mon 24
(G) CHRISTMAS EVE SPECIAL HOLIDAY MATINEE for the young of all ages (open 1:30)
SCROOGE musical adaptation of Dicken's "Christmas Carol! Albert Finney4only
SNOOPY COME HOME very best of the Peanuts gang.full-lenth animated cartoon2

Tue 25
(G) PACIFIC VIBRATIONS the best surfing-music film ever.the global surfer!7,11
THE WHITE SEARCH one man's seach for the skiing paradise, a feature-film by
Dick Barrington,filmed in Austria,Aspen,Chile,Italy,Hawaii,Sun Valley,etc9
PLUS:award-winning featurette "Sail in the Surf"(Catamaran) & surprise4short

Thu 27
(G) THE GOLD RUSH Charlie Chaplin's best feature-length film.work of genious 9
THE GENERAL (1926) starring & directed by Buster Keaton.the Civil War 7,11
PLUS: Two Charlie Chaplin Two-reelers:"The Immigrant," and "Easy Street"

Fri 28
(R) BEYOND THE VALLEY OF THE PREVUES a hallucinatory 90 minutes of the most
nerve-breaking,nostalgic,classic,&amazing trailers of film-history's once-
coming attractions. a thrill every 3.7 seconds! many vintage goldens! 8:30
FREAKS (1938) the original suppressed masterpiece of the macabre. 7 & 11
ACID CAMP (31 min) country-boy goes to S.F. for kicks, and ends up on acid,
seduced by three voluptuous hippie maidens. slapstik-psychedelia-sex 10:30

Sat 29
(X) FRITZ THE CAT Robert Crumb's immortal feline is X-rated and animated! 7,11
YELLOW SUBMARINE the Beatles,Blue Meanies,animation-lightshow tripper 9only

Cumberland Mountain Theaters, Inc.

146

Greg, Marti and me

The downside was another thing. Story manuscripts coming back in self-addressed stamped envelopes with boiler-plate rejection slips. Too many careless romances ending in too many people hurt. The hollowing pit in my stomach whenever I thought of my father; or, tell the truth, whenever I didn't think of him, which was almost always. Why? Because I knew too little even to wonder about such unspoken family matters, and thus that worming inside, and the movies, and books, helping me pretend to ignore it...

Post-AFI, while Greg and I banged away at one generic spec script after another—western, war, screwball, thriller—Marti went to work hustling set director jobs all over town. She was good, and reliable, and she kept getting hired; until one day the phone rang and it was Marti calling to ask if I was free for the next few weeks. There was this independent feature about to start up out in the Valley and she was going to be needing an assistant? And presto: my next job.

The wink-wink title of this first quickie was *Every Girl Should Have One*, a brainless diamond-heist caper picture starring Miss Hungary of 1936, late-night talk-show celeb Zsa Zsa Gabor.

My job on set was to pay attention, stay out of the way, and move things around whenever Marti gave me the high sign. Mindless labor for the most part but plenty of it, plus the schedule was a bear, pre-dawn to past dark, the whole cast and crew working our asses off when we weren't waiting around for the next shot. This included Zsa Zsa, all hairspray and chiffon and breathy off-camera requests, *Dahlink, with those eyes, I'm dying of thirst,* my cue to fetch another glass of chilled Perrier so she could bat those false lashes and pucker up for the first sip. But with a witless screenplay guiding the way and rock-bottom production values, the resulting movie stank out loud. You could look it up on YouTube.

Our next job was no improvement. *The Bees* stooped, and I mean low, to rip off this big-budget hit from the previous year that had cashed in on the dread then sweeping the land of a rumored invasion from south of the border by swarms of Africanized killer bees. Our stripped-down, sexed-up version featured a stolid John Saxon and sultry costar Angel Tompkins, still shapely, still honey blonde though at a certain tightlipped remove from her pouting glory days in *Playboy.* [2]

They Prey on HUMAN FLESH!

the BEES

Starring **JOHN SAXON · ANGEL TOMPKINS · JOHN CARRADINE**
Music by RICHARD GILLIS · Director of Photography: LEON SANCHEZ
Written, Directed and Produced by ALFREDO ZACHARIAS

    By now, I was given to understand, my title had been inflated to assistant prop master, a promotion that meant little more than gofer though I was pressed into doing special-effects chores when the shoot's makeup artist, citing cause, refused. [3] Chores as in, drive around greater Los Angeles emptying every Big Five sporting goods store of its stock of McGinty wet flies, feather-and-chenille concoctions in beelike black and yellow favored by warm-water panfish anglers; snip off barbs down to hook shank; and using flexible rubber cement and every ounce of forbearance, apply by the dozens to the face of our leading lady. For her closeup.

On orders from the AD this side job-within-a-job played out in an unmoving freight elevator with the doors shut tight to muffle the uproar inside as with pricked, sticky fingers I glued on bug after bug and the apoplectic Miss Angel raged.

And yet, strange, isn't it, the pleasure we can take recollecting such unpleasantries, given the sorcery of time? It's something like that upswelling both/and superabundance afforded us by film itself, one thing becoming something else again, the real and the unreal and the hyperreal all combining, the past, the present, even the as-yet unlived future unspooling before our eyes in the irresistible flow lavished on us through the story world up there on screen; and the only filmic constant, as in the rest of life at large, change upon change upon change…

The last time Marti called to ask if I was available for another job things had changed, big time, for her. After cutting her teeth on several of the sorriest products ever churned out by Hollywood's open-shop meat-grinding other self, she was now working for Orson Welles.

All dogs except for one.

I'm not sure what images the name Orson Welles might conjure up among young people today, or if to them the name means anything at all. In the mid-1970s it was inextricably linked to Welles's audacious first feature, *Citizen Kane*, the 1941 drama that at the age of 25 the preternaturally gifted Boy Wonder (a newspaper nickname he detested) cowrote, produced, directed, and starred in, and that for generations would be hailed as the greatest work of cinema in the medium's history. [4]

None of which would save Welles from falling out of favor with the powerbrokers of American film. Too much his own man, too much an artist, and too much trouble for all that, before the 1950s were over he was shut out forever from mainstream Hollywood filmmaking, condemned to going his own way.

151

And thus from the sublime to the ridiculous, *Citizen Kane*, *The Bees*, and *Every Girl Should Have One* sharing space in the same off-kilter reminiscence. If the grouping appears unlikely, believe me, Scout's honor, the world was a different place back then.

For example, in addition to hiring on to design and build a set for the hush-hush new project that Orson Welles—*Orson Welles!*—was mounting to announce his Hollywood return after years of self-exile in Europe, Marti confided that she was also accompanying the man himself onto various television talk and variety shows—as the shill in his magic act. Her role? Pretending to be a clueless member of the audience when, as if at random, she was selected to come onstage and have her mind read.

Once up there, after the requisite magician banter and mystic hand jive, often involving a silken blindfold, Marti would recite the word or phrase that they had rehearsed while from thin air, or behind her ear, or the inner leaves of some stage-prop doorstopper, Welles would unfold an innocent-looking scrap of paper just so inscribed, to the gasping amazement of all.

Friday's best

Orson Welles on "The Magic of David Copperfield."

7:00 p.m. ② **THE MAGIC OF DAVID COPPERFIELD.** David Copperfield and celebrity guest magicians perform acts of the seemingly impossible in a music and comedy format. Carl Ballantine, Valerie Bertinelli, Sherman Hemsley, Bernadette Peters, Orson Welles, and Cindy Williams guest-star.

Marti, in the middle, with Mr. Welles

You won't find any of this in Josh Karp's *Orson Welles's Last Movie: The Making of 'The Other Side of the Wind'*. [5] The book tells a fabulous story, quintessentially Wellesian in the sweep and coil and outright chutzpah of it all, and Karp does an admirable job tracing out the saga of that long, jinxed production; but Marti isn't in it, and I wish she were.

I get why she's not. From later experience as a biographer, experience no more imaginable in 1975 than had I gone on to win the Olympic marathon, or rob liquor stores, or finally find my father, I know the impossibility of tracking down and recording, much less including in the narrative, every thread of any life, much less the background life of such an epically complicated film as *The Other Side of the Wind*.

But Marti was my friend, and not long ago she died, and though doubtless it's too little, too late, I believe she deserves to be remembered for having worked as closely and

153

as curiously as she did with Orson Welles through such a strange and exhilarating and yes crushing time. [6]

Me, I was there too, if only briefly, along with my younger brother Gino, who came and went. [7] True, all I did was answer Marti's call for somebody to cut lumber and pound nails on the backyard tennis court at 628 North Hillcrest, the Beverly Hills mansion that Peter Bogdanovich had rented for Welles. But I was there, and so was Oja Kodar, Orson's knockout Croatian partner-paramour-cowriter-star, sunbathing by the pool to maintain a dazzling full-body tan for her role as the film's mysterious, often naked Native American sex goddess.

Not that I knew at the time what her role was. Beyond the immediate work at hand Marti and I were told little to nothing about the film, and only decades later did the particulars come to light. But there was Oja poolside, hard by the tennis court, turning over when done on one side to even out the equally distracting other.

The tennis court was where we assembled the parts of the set we were building, one section at a time. Our assignment was to suggest the interior corner of a nightclub restroom consisting of countertop, sink, and adjacent wall mirrors. Simple enough job, it might seem. But Orson Welles was nothing if not an exacting taskmaster. Reduced to working even this far from the full-service sound stages of his wunderkind beginnings at RKO, he still insisted on his vision being realized down to the last detail.

And so Marti and I would show up in the morning and work through the day, sawing, hammering, remeasuring to make adjustments. And then, late in the afternoon, Mr. Welles would emerge from the house in flowing purple robe to make his daily tour of our progress.

As he padded around the structure puffing on a gigantic cigar, stroking his beard, *barefoot*, I couldn't stop myself from sneaking glances at the sheer tremendousness of his girth, from the side, from the rear, but mostly at the astounding, alarming vertical mass of his feet, great slabs of flesh all but absent of ankle and a bafflement how they could ever be wedged into shoes. Embarrassing, I admit, but how could I help it? I could hardly believe I was standing on a netless green tennis court of all places, next to Orson Welles of all people, awestruck as much by the legend of his life's work as by the sheer magnitude of the physical man; and without a snapshot to prove it—answers fail when yet again the question arises why I never thought to bring my drugstore Instamatic and take one of the three of us, or better yet the four, Oja too—what can I do but show you through my eyes what I remember.

Near the end of the week Gary Graver started showing up to take part in these inspections. Gary was Welles's cinematographer, a steadfast disciple and dedicated craftsman but also a slave to the wages he drew shooting skin flick after skin flick, *The Naughty Stewardesses*, *The Dirty Dolls*, *Girls for Rent*, and so on. He and Orson would confer, Gary looking more or less worn out but attending closely to the give-and-take between them and Marti while I stood back awaiting instructions; until the day came to move the various parts of our construction into the pool house for their all-important camera test.

Once Marti and I had secured the counter and the sink and anchored the two wall mirrors on their marks, Gary finessed the lights, glanced through the viewfinder of his Arriflex, and stepped aside. You could hear Mr. Welles breathing as he bent down to look. Cigar smoke curling ceilingward, he looked hard and long before lifting his great lion's head to double-check something, then lowered his gaze to peer again.

Whatever he saw must have looked somehow wrong for in the next moment he straightened up and loomed, coming at me where I stood off to one side of the set trying my best in the cramped space to make way. I backed up a step, then another, retreating into shadow until I was stumbling, lurching sideways, tangled up in extension cords and sandbags and watching as if in nightmare slow motion one whole framed wall of our set came crashing down.

155

Then silence, and our breathing, the four of us.

My first impulse was to check for blood, not mine but Orson's, on the floor where the mirror had shattered; and for once, thank God, he was wearing slippers. Less comforting was the way he stood there breathing, in and out, on the point I was sure of exploding. I braced myself, knowing he had every right—I was supposed to be building something, not demolishing it, then burning up from shame—and yet for some reason he held back.

Faced with the loss of an entire day from his life's work, probably more than one day, who knew, but the thing he lived for, making movies out of dust and spit and wizardry, he was patient, even gracious in the willed aplomb of his restraint; and when it was clear we had all survived, shaken but in one piece, he rolled his shoulders, gave us a look, and retraced his steps back into the house as much as if to say *Tomorrow then,* or *Art is long,* or *We get it, kid: chin up;* Gary Graver departed for the night; and Marti helped me sweep up the wreckage.

A moment from the making of Orson Welles's last film, banal and no doubt meaningless except to the guy who still feels the scald of it, and the lasting shock of unexpected generosity…

The next day Marti and I returned to rebuild what I had ruined, and the next day after that; and when at last the repairs met with Mr. Welles's approval, our job was finished.

Still unfinished a decade later when Orson Welles died at age 70, *The Other Side of the Wind* entered the realm of myth. Of all the projects he left in pieces for the future to puzzle over—*It's All True, Moby Dick, The Deep, One Man Band, The Dreamers, Orson Welles's Magic Show, King Lear*— this one became the biggest what-if of all, nearly 100 hours of raw footage plus a mountain of roughly edited scenes, marked-up scripts, and director's memos to self and others. And then? And then it was all locked up and left to languish

156

in a Paris vault while for the next several decades attorneys, financiers, family members, and assorted filmmakers strived, vied, wrangled, and fought over what could or should or must be done, or not, and how, and when, and where, and through it all with whose put-up-or-shut-up money. Those were a few of the questions.

It wasn't until 2018, nearly half a century after principal photography had commenced, that the world finally got its answer. Thanks to the doggedness of a few true believers, chief among them producers Frank Marshall and Jan Filip Rymsza, and the funds generated by a successful Indiegogo drive, Netflix announced the release of their painstaking reconstruction of the film, "an attempt to honor and complete [Welles's] vision."

Marti hadn't lived to witness the event, so I was all the keener to see what had become of our collaboration, and how it fit into the film's larger design.

The Other Side of the Wind tells the story of the last day in the life of acclaimed veteran filmmaker Jake Hannaford, played with knowing brio by Welles friend and fellow alpha director John Huston, fresh from his role as the fiendish Noah Cross in *Chinatown*. Hailed as the Ernest Hemingway of the cinema—whose studio contracts stipulate that he gets to shoot, to death, the animals in his films, and whose father, like Hemingway's, has died by his own hand—Hannaford shows up for his seventieth birthday party besieged by scores of admirers, critics, old friends, and new rivals come to pay their respects or, less charitably, to provoke a rise from the guest of honor.

The party is being hosted by Zarah Valeska (the luminous Lilli Palmer), one of Hannaford's stars from bygone days though never yet one of his conquests. Humoring Hannaford's current overtures and acting only out of friendship, Zarah wants to put the director in touch with the new generation, for, as she gently phrases it, "Most people of [his] age are too old for him." Left unspoken is the suggestion that indeed he may have fallen out of touch, and the possibility that this is making him anxious. But no need to say so when Hannaford's mounting disquiet becomes all too visible, triggered by those among the celebrants who detect the life-or-death struggle being waged beneath his trademark bravado—the struggle to avoid being swept aside by the rising wave of an upstart New Hollywood embodied by golden-boy director and self-anointed Hannaford "apostle" Brooks Otterlake (Peter Bogdanovich, oozing baby-faced charm and killer oedipal instincts).

Will Hannaford succeed? With few signposts to guide the way through layers of ever-more meta fiction, we are drawn on by suspense as our two main storylines shift back and forth, from straightforward footage of the celebration being shot by several verité documentarians, to fever-dream portions of the experimental film Hannaford is making to jumpstart his comeback. These fragments are being screened as the centerpiece of the party, cinematic snippets in no discernible order: chase scenes, sex scenes, panoramic vistas featuring two enigmatic figures, the unnamed Actress (Oja Kodar) and her costar the actor John Dale (Bob Random). But with too many "Missing Shot" cards interrupting the haphazardness, not a word of dialogue spoken by either character, and their performances verging on the wooden— as well as one, two, three power outages cutting off the projection for increasingly ominous comic relief—the sense grows that Hannaford has not only lost touch with the right people, he's also lost his director's touch as one of the world's leading filmmakers. By the end of the night he will learn that the production is bankrupt, that going on with it will be impossible. His film's title too: *The Other Side of the Wind*.

So, an indisputably once-great director, Orson Welles, scrambling late in life to reestablish himself, makes a film about a once-great director, the fictional Jake Hannaford, late in his life scrambling, etc. We are in story-within-storyworld, self-reflexive movie-within-movieland, where mirrors and mirroring proliferate.

158

Early on in his career, and not once but twice for good measure, Orson Welles had set the standard for how to stage a successful mirror scene. The first time occurred in *Citizen Kane*, where the once-imperious Charles Foster Kane, now a broken man, trudges past the endless mirror-to-mirror reflection of himself trudging, as if endlessly, toward his undoing. The second time, more ingenious still, was the climactic Magic Mirror Maze shootout in *The Lady from Shanghai* (1947), where it's impossible to differentiate the real from its reflection, with inevitable, fatal results.

The Other Side of the Wind does its fair share of playing with mirrors too. Consider the scene, well described by Karp, where Welles filmed Huston as Hannaford unleashing "a drunken, self-loathing monologue upon himself in a bathroom mirror [with] the kind of intimacy usually reserved for young actresses' nude scenes..." [8]

159

THE MAKING OF
THE OTHER SIDE
OF THE WIND

ORSON • • • • • • • • • • •
• • • • • WELLES'S
LAST M●VIE
• • • • • • • • • • • • • JOSH KARP • •

Or the mirror scene without a mirror, where priggish English teacher Dr. Burroughs (Dan Tobin) enters the party momentarily befuddled by an empty picture frame, on the other side of which a fellow partygoer aiming a handheld movie camera apes the professor's movements, mirror-like.

And then there's the other bathroom scene, the one containing the set with mirrors that Marti and I built and built again. In spite of itself the scene is one to remember, even if not for those mirrors, which appear to reflect nothing of significance. Or could that be their point? For in a film teeming with outré images, careening cuts, and entire passages that on first viewing can defy comprehension— Hannaford's film-within-a-film, that is—this scene offers one of the most inscrutable moments of all.

It takes place against the backdrop of a parallel party going on inside the Hannaford film, louder and raunchier in a forced 1970s B-movie kind of way than the actual birthday gathering. Psychedelic lights pulsate in lurid Technicolor. Longhaired extras gyrate to ersatz acid rock. Voluptuous women abound both in the flesh and the porn being projected on background walls.

And then we are inside the bathroom with the Actress, walking slowly along the tiles in a tracking shot that reveals sybarites galore in a variety of genders going at it with each other in the toilet stalls while staring daggers at her (and us) as she passes. Dripping wet herself—she has just been thrown out of the car where she too was going at it with her impassive costar, steamy scene, no question, and raining cats and dogs—The Actress strips down to the sheerest of slips then removes even that to toss, unaccountably, at an unaccountable young woman perched on the sink in front of those two reconstructed mirrors of ours.

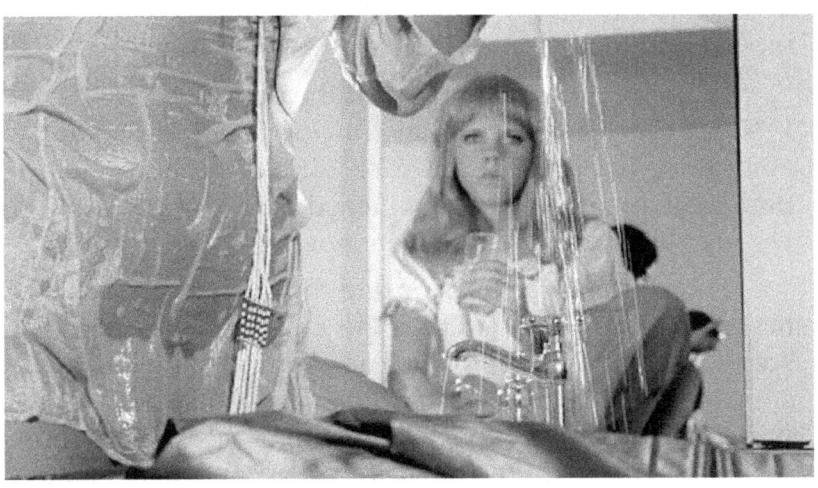

Oja Kodar in wet slip as The Actress, Teresa Nersesyan on sink as Ice Cube Girl, and the mirror wall that had to be rebuilt (Netflix).

Designated Ice Cube Girl in the credits, this young woman (Teresa Nerseyan) is enjoying a fizzing glass of Fresca, Welles's favorite diet soda, as if expressly waiting for the damp undergarment to land on her lap so she can pull it over her face and inhale. The fabric sucks into the cavity of her mouth, lending her the aspect of a living, breathing death mask; and then she sticks, really sticks out a red, red tongue to strain, yep, phallically, against the resistant winding-sheet veil.

Not the come-hither gesture likeliest to succeed, it turns out, for the Actress's response, fair to call chilly, is to zip herself up into a shiny black raincoat, pluck an ice cube from the glass, and jam it down Ice Cube Girl's shrouded throat.

Huh? Come again? Say what?

Okay, but gauzy underthings, black rubber raincoat, close-up flashes of attractive body parts—sexy, right? Well, hardly, just two minutes' screen time of gratuitous, self-conscious overkill and scene over, no resonance, no depth, no artful reflection shots to supply much less underline some or any meaning, just two mirrors at right angles adding up to a tawdry sense of place for this tawdry slice of kink to play out in. [9]

To say I was disappointed the first time I watched Welles's film, only to see how little our work ended up amounting to, would be an honest if mortifying understatement. But then I watched it all again and, wonderful to say, my eyes were opened.

You see, those mirrors and the missed opportunity to make something of them, like the general misfire of the entire scene, are exactly what Welles needed to certify Hannaford's slippage—and Welles's own ravishing command. The paradox is a glorious one, for in turning the camera upon his own fictionalized reflection as recorded by what Hannaford calls "the eye" of "the magic box," and as projected back through the play acting of John Huston (reflections always amounting to something else again), Welles manages to have it both ways. If anything, *The Other Side of the Wind* demands to be seen as displaying a level of thematic ambition bolder even than *Citizen Kane*, because here it is so much closer to home: no safely iconoclastic assault upon such an easy public target as William Randolph Hearst, but the confession of an artist's own deepest private doubts and weaknesses, even as he asserts his profoundest strengths.

In short, throughout what we see of Hannaford's film we are inside the vision of a man who is no longer an insider, no longer in touch, an old man up against his own impending mortality and the brutal limits of his moviemaking artistry—and so he is badly overreaching. Yes, his film does have its moments hinting of erstwhile genius: the metronomic intensity of that rain-drenched sex scene; the swirling end-of-days portent in all that wind. But no matter how great Hannaford may have been for the lion's share of his career, he has been away too long, the world has moved on, and now all he can do is grin that wolfish grin, keep swilling scotch, hustle the youngest girl (Cathy Lucas) he can lay hands on, and blast away at a grotesque shooting gallery of papier-mâché effigies depicting his pretty-boy leading man.

"He looks like a girl," says the disgusted studio executive (Geoffrey Land) suffering through rushes of Hannaford's much-anticipated work in progress before standing up and walking out. "Tell Jake"—he's talking to Hannaford's factotum Billy Boyle, played to backsliding dried-out alcoholic perfection by old-time Welles collaborator Norman Foster, and the message is an order, not a comment—"Tell Jake he wasted my time." [10]

A pretty picture this isn't but it does speak the truth. Hannaford's time is behind him, the time of the big game-hunting international auteur and lady killer, the truth about him exposed by the radical ambivalence blazing forth from the core of his film about who he might really be beneath all that swaggering public persona.

Here the Hemingway connection grows even more apt, and who could have seen it coming? For among several works left unfinished when the Nobel laureate ended his own life with a double-barreled shotgun to the forehead—

July 2, 1961, note the date—was the typescript of *The Garden of Eden*, unpublished until a heavily reconstructed edition of the novel appeared a quarter century later with its image-busting exploration of fluid man-woman gender roles and their uncentered, decentering mutability.

And not only that. Look again and the biblical reference of Hemingway's title—*The Garden of Eden*—only extends the intertextual web of connections informing *The Other Side of the Wind*. For who but John Huston had directed *The Bible: In the Beginning*, his 1966 cast-of-thousands epic covering the first twenty-two chapters of the Book of Genesis, with uncredited script work by Orson Welles, and Huston himself performing the offscreen voice of God. And now, at the birthday party, it's about God himself that Hannaford's most acute critic, the Pauline Kael-ish Miss Rich (Susan Strasberg, all tenacity), makes her way through the crowd to confront him.

What about God? she asks. How does He fit into the club or clan or members-only clique of powerful male figures that Hannaford helps define?

"*She*," Hannaford drily corrects her. "We're all ruled by the wind, aren't we, lady? So, if the Lord is a lady, and God's will is her will, then we can all relax and stop expecting the universe to be logical."

God in the whirlwind: that's bedrock Old Testament, as fundamental to the recognition that life's central organizing principle may be chaos as Aristophanes's pronouncement that *Zeus is dethroned, and Whirl is king.* [11] Take your pick. Either way, it's a terrifying choice—God exists or does not exist and still, chaos reigns—a recognition that only makes Hannaford laugh as he embraces it.

"Just like me and God," he baits Miss Rich, teasing out the dark fun that can be had with cases of mistaken identity. "If it weren't for the difference in sex how could you tell us apart?"

Good question, among plenty of others. For example, driving away from the aftermath of the party at dawn the next morning in that lethal-looking Porsche convertible, does Hannaford crash and die by his own hand, intentionally, or owing to King Chaos, by accident, and on the second of July of all dates? And John Huston's bleak voiceover through the final seconds of Welles's film, as Hannaford's film plays out in the far background on the screen of a desolate, deserted drive-in—are we meant to take that voice as some kind of annihilating Last Word, an anti-gospel of despair, or as a harbinger of things yet unseen, of resurrectionist possibilities addressed to us as if from beyond the grave and, if so, doesn't that mean he still lives? Listen:

"Who knows, maybe you can stare too hard at something, huh? Drain out the virtue, suck out the living juice. You shoot the great places and the pretty people. All those girls and boys. Shoot 'em dead."

Maybe it does sound like the voice of some godforsaken death god, like the specter of the terrible deity Miss Rich raises in front of the whole party when she dresses Hannaford down to his barest, calling him out for his compulsion to destroy everything he creates—for which he will strike her, and who can forgive him for that?

Questions to come back to, no doubt. Suffice it to say that the first time I watched *The Other Side of the Wind* I barely made it through to the end, so utterly did I misconstrue it. Blinded by the hunt for the set that I had helped build so many years earlier, I mistook the failure of Hannaford's desperate last-ditch efforts for that of Orson Welles; when in fact Hannaford's failure bespeaks Welles's triumph, a masterful do-over of the battle he had so often waged, the battle against mediocrity and Hollywood group think and above all chaos, transformed into ultimate, if posthumous control.

Fortunately, I tried again, and with each repeated viewing, surface blemishes aside, I now see how the myriad parts of the film all fit together in a magnificent, moving act of artistic magic and revelation, ineffable in the richness of its

165

total effect—in the words of Richard Brody, "a belated work of… colossal artistry." [12]

Of course, strictly speaking, in a world where change is the only constant, there's no such thing as repetition; and so there remains the next viewing to look forward to, and the next after that, and each time more to see, and more clearly.

"This famous old lion of yours is not what you think."

So says longtime Hannaford screenwriter The Baron (the stately Tonio Selwart), like Zarah Velaska an immigrant from the Old World and likewise one of *The Other Side of the Wind*'s most trustworthy voices: "I'd call him a necromancer but I don't know if he's raised the dead."

Metaphorically speaking, can we agree that necromancy, the dark art of summoning the spirits of the dead, must be one of film's most powerful attractors? Or perhaps not so metaphorically; for what other medium preserves the very light and shadow and timbre and gait of the people it records, not to mention, at its best, film's capacity for intimating deeper, more inward qualities, the stuff—the spirit—of their personhood? Certain observers of realist film, Bazin, perhaps Kracauer, go so far as to equate the material object itself—the emulsified strip of celluloid imprinted with so much light—with the reflecting source of that light, human or otherwise, in a miracle of ontological identity: the river flowing and still flowing through Renoir's *A Day in the Country*, for example, or Dryer's Joan of Arc and that immortalized fly forever alighting on her radiant, suffering face. [13]

Think too hard about this stuff and you can risk spooking yourself, all the legions of the dead who live and love and fight and dance and kill and yes die on film, only to live again. But give yourself over to the movies and there they are, ever patient, waiting to be summoned and revived…

Twenty-some years after the year I worked with Marti, I came up for a decent job. I was on the far side of forty with a wife and two kids and still working hand-to-mouth, no longer in horseshoe-counter cafes or on teetering paint-spattered ladders, but across the southland, season to season, in so many freeway-flyer college classrooms. At last now before me was an interview offering the prospect of a much-needed upgrade in terms both professional and personal, and so I prepped and practiced and memorized the lines of my make-or-break job talk; in the middle of which I got lost.

Straying from a sober academic discussion of film history and film theory and the most effective pedagogies of teaching film, etc., I found myself telling how I had once worked for Orson Welles, and how I messed up with that mirror. And when the story broke off all I could feel was how bad I had blown it, bullet-in-the-brain fatally, it felt like.

Strange to say, I got the job. Stranger still, getting it made me feel like I was finally finished with my twenties and climbing into a life of my own. From which point the next step felt not only necessary but fated, and like the gravest of obligations: I set out on the search for my father.

Not that I thought I would find him. Finding him wasn't the goal. He was dead, I knew that much, disappearing from my life when I was young enough to remember little more than a faceless man-shadow receding into some fearsome distance, and the too-familiar sense of a hovering absence at the center of most everything else. Because of the shame at that time associated with mental illness and suicide, he passed from death into unspeakable family secret, the strongest lock box in the annals of the human heart as shown forth in literature, in film, again and again, from *Oedipus Rex* to yes *Chinatown* and beyond. Such stories, I had learned, offer few happy endings; but whatever was out there to discover that might help me start filling in some blanks, I needed to go seeking. And this need scared me down to my bones.

Long story short, that search brought me and my brother Gino to the doorstep in another city of our father's only surviving sibling. I had not seen our Uncle Ted since I was too young to recall and contact between the two sides of the family had been severed, so despite our shared blood and all that once was, to each other now we were strangers.

When Gino and I pulled up at the curb Ted and his wife, our aunt, were waiting. We got out of the car introducing ourselves and they stood on the lawn looking back at us. They stood there looking, more and more closely, before coming forward a step, saying how much of Joe they could see in the both of us, another step, but in Stephen especially, his eyes, the way he stands with his hands in his pockets; and our aunt reaching out to touch my ear, my cheekbone, and then welcoming us into their home.

We joined them in the living room and talked. Our aunt served coffee and homemade sweets and they told stories about our father, about his musical talent, his tool-and-diemaker skills, his love of the mountains and the ocean and his sleek little inboard runabout *Joey's Joy*. And when it was clear we had all been waiting through much of our lives for this moment, they presented us with gifts of two other things he had loved, his Winchester pump-action 12-gauge shotgun, freshly oiled, and his violin in its leather case with a program from the recital where he had performed the "Méditation" from *Thaïs*. (14)

Uncle Ted excused himself. When he returned he was rolling a vintage 8-mm projector with a cardboard box full of old home movies. He hadn't shown these films in a long, long time, he warned us, and he was afraid they might break or burn up, but he and our aunt both thought we should see them....

The long, largely silent drive from Los Angeles to get there. The apprehension as we had approached. After so many years of knowing so little it all felt like a dream as our uncle, my godfather, drew the shades, dimmed the lights and toggled the On switch, and the reels began to turn.

Psychologists conjecture that cases of chronic excessive shame can originate from the loss of a parent's love, for in the child's distorted view that loss is their fault. Because shame-based behavior can thus function as an unconscious attempt to preserve the attachment, such trauma can have long-lasting adverse effects that nevertheless can be treated and healed. If the loss occurs at a very early age, healing must address the loss experience itself with acknowledgement, empathy, and good faith. [15]

The films, it turned out, did not break or burn up and my brother and I sat watching, enthralled to see our father alive again. Gripping saltwater rod and gleaming bonito. With waxed wooden skis heading back upslope. As best man in tails and boutonnière at Ted and Shirley's wedding. In grease-flecked machinist's apron at work. And, most piercing of all, outside in the sun holding Gino and me up in either arm, beaming, while I aimed my six-shooter at whoever might be gazing back from the unimaginable future, father and sons on a lost forgotten day in all our reflected still-shining light.

Which leaves us with the mysteries, whatever those might be, given our individual singularities. Orson Welles's Jake Hannaford has his:

"Friendship and movies," Hannaford says. "Those are mysteries."

And Zarah Valeska: "Durability. It can be rather fragile sometimes. To keep that feeling we need to keep our distance."

To which the briefly hopeful Hannaford, chastened, replies with equal parts irony and goodwill, "Thanks, mother."

My friend Greg left LA a while back but we still get together whenever we can to stalk trout and swap lines from *The Wild Bunch*. Like Marti, our other friend from AFI days died too, *Walk the Line* screenwriter Gill Dennis, and too many others besides, among them John Huston, whose first film, *The Maltese Falcon*, premiered the same year as *Citizen Kane*, that matchless pair of mysteries, and whose last film, *The Dead*, from James Joyce's great story, Huston directed while dying himself, at once protest and assent and homage and soaring gift, the way that art can also be offering...

Today, Sunday, December 20, 2020, our Uncle Ted died too. He was 89 years old and he died of the coronavirus, albeit peacefully, thank God. After being separated for most of our lives we were reunited in no small part through the uncanny humanity of film, and in the end we had twenty good years.

And now there's that box of home movies and loose photos to keep sifting through, holding negatives up to the lamplight until some other blur from the past leaps into focus. A shard of clarity out of the chaos. The other side of the wind.

[1] See Andrew O'Hehir, "Rape, Power and Polanski's *Chinatown*." *Salon* (October 13, 2009),

https://www.salon.com/2009/10/13/chinatown/ [accessed August 7, 2021].

2 *Playboy*, February 1972.

3 Despite that word-of-mouth promotion the movie's end credits reflected no such thing.

4 In contrast to the suggestion of David Fincher's *Mank* (2020) that Welles did little if any writing on the script for *Citizen Kane*, see Thomas Stackpole, "Who Really Wrote *Citizen Kane*?" *Smithsonian Magazine* (May 2016), https://www.smithsonianmag.com/history/who-really-wrote-citizen-kane-180958782/ [accessed December 16, 2020].

5 Josh Karp, Orson Welles's Last Movie: The Making of 'The Other Side of the Wind'. New York: St. Martin's Press, 2015.

6 Part of the curiosity comes across in Marti's comment when she wrote me to say, "I had just started working for Orson when he received that AFI award. They warned me not to mention my AFI Fellowship because Orson hated film schools and film students. Haha!" LinkedIn message, May 14, 2015. For the story of how the award tribute went awry for Welles, see Karp, 180-189.

7 Gino, far handier than his big brother, joined us for a few days with his pickup, his tools, and his good-humored know-how.

8 Karp, 136.

9 For background insight into this scene, see Ray Kelly, "Ice Cube Girl Recalls *The Other Side of the Wind* Shoot." https://www.wellesnet.com/ice-cube-girl-other-side-wind/ [accessed January 2, 2021].

10 Writer-director Norman Foster teamed up with Welles when, immediately following *Citizen Kane*, they plunged into the ill-fated 1941 omnibus *It's All True*. Collaborating with fellow screenwriter John Fante, Foster adapted a story by documentarian Robert J. Flaherty about a Mexican boy and a fighting bull, one of four parts that Welles planned for the film. Their script went into production in Mexico with Foster directing but before he could finish, the entire project was canceled. For Welles Fante also wrote on his own the script for what would have been the film's fourth segment, "Love Story," loosely based on his immigrant parents' courtship and including an amusement-park funhouse scene worth a closer comparative look vis-à-vis the Magic Mirror Maze climax of *The Lady from Shanghai*.

[11] *"God in the whirlwind"*: See the books of Job, Isaiah, Jeremiah, etc. *"Whirl is king"*: Aristophanes, *The Clouds*.

[12] Richard Brody, *"The Other Side of the Wind, Reviewed: A Belated Orson Welles Masterpiece." The New Yorker*, November 2, 2018.

[13] André Bazin, "The Ontology of the Photographic Image," in *What Is Cinema?*, vol. 1. Hugh Gray, trans. Berkeley: University of California Press, 1967. Siegfried Kracauer, *Theory of Film: The Redemption of Physical Reality*. New York: Oxford University Press, 1960.

[14] Adapted from the 1890 novel by Anatole France, Jules Massenet's opera caused a scandal on opening in 1894 for its dramatic treatment of religious eroticism. The story traces the struggles of devout monk Athanaël to convert the sensuous courtesan Thaïs to Christianity, only to expose in the end his lustful motives while revealing her inner goodness.

[15] https://traumaticstressinstitute.org/wp-content/files_mf/1276631745ShameandAttachment.pdf [accessed December 16, 2020].

Kendall Johnson

Heroes, Strength, Time and Kirk Douglas

Growing up in the 50s in small-town Claremont, California, my several friends and I took refuge from the summer heat in the air-conditioned Village Theater downtown. Popcorn was buttered and fresh, cokes were cheap, and the Abba Zaba taffy and peanut butter bars could pull out fillings at ten paces. Ushers smiled and picked up trash. There were double features, news reels, cartoons. Script writers churned out stories, mostly simple, but entertaining in a mindless sort of way. We ate it up.

Good guys wore the white hats, bad guys the black, and the issues were never complex. The virtuous stood up against evil, and women were victims to be saved. Robert Mitchum, Burt Lancaster, William Holden, and John Wayne, all taught us to be ready to fight the Nazis, Communists, and Indians. Kirk Douglas played it all, starring in *The Vikings*, *Spartacus*, and *Paths of Glory*.

Back then, the Second World War had been won, Korea forgotten, and Vietnam was still in pre-production phase. We were taught to put down our cap pistols and chaps, trade in our cowboy hats for battle helmets. To be proper men, that's what we did, and signed up for Khe Sahn, Vihn Moc, and the Ia Drang Valley. Later, when we returned from Vietnam confused and broken, when Camelot crashed and it became less clear just who were the good or bad, and who was or wasn't brave, Hollywood's black and white turned inside out and into muddled shades of gray.

Flash forward a half-century or so, and we are still looking for direction and comfort, but are finding less and less. Movie theaters still pull in numbers of us who seeking refrigeration, popcorn and candy, and stories that—however fanciful, or spectacular, or even apocalyptic—still reassure us that all will work out in the end.

Yet in the back of our minds we become more and more troubled. Newscasters whisper rumors that all might not be well, that worse wars are coming, the economy will crash, that water is becoming short, and the earth and air are rapidly breaking down. Words no longer even mean the same to different people. Deep in our hearts we look for simple reassurance, we still hunger for sitting in the dark together, eating popcorn, all looking in one direction.

The Year is 2020: Adventure writer Sebastian Junger sits alone at the Au Rendez-Vous des Belges, just across from the Gare du Nord, as instructed. The somewhat disembodied voice over his hotel phone had claimed to be Kirk Douglas' ghost. It was early in the evening so he'd decided to see what was behind all the mysterious cloak and dagger.

A couple gets up and moves over to his table. "Excuse me," the man reaches out to shake Sebastian's hand, "I'm Kirk Douglas." And he was. "Thank you for coming, I'd like to introduce you to Ms. Andrée De Jongh."

"I'm glad to meet you, Mr. Junger," said Andrée, shaking his hand. "I've been keeping up on your adventure journalism."

Shaking her hand, Sebastian looks more closely. "I've heard your name before."

"Ms. De Jongh was twenty-three years old when the Nazis invaded her country, Belgium," Kirk Douglas explains. "This 100-pound girl led soldiers and airmen south 600 miles through enemy held territory, across the Pyrenees to the British consulate in Bilbao."

"Look," Sebastian holds up a hand. "you've come to tell me hero stories about WWII? This is 2020."

"Yes, it is, Sebastian," Andrée replies. "You write adventure stories, showing people doing courageous things. It is now time for you to talk about the real heroes, the ones who get up every day facing a world they no longer recognize."

174

"You refer to the political situation, the fear? The new Nazis? Or the cyber-anonymity?"

"All of it." Kirk smiles. "It reminds me of a conversation I had with John Wayne once, early in my career, about being macho. I told him, if I play a strong man in a film, I look for the moments where he's weak. And if I play a weak character, I look for the moments where he's strong because that's what drama's all about—chiaroscuro, light and shade."

"Mr. Junger, the real battle you folks are going to be waging in the next few years is the battle for hope, and I'm glad I don't have to be around. But you are, and if you are going to show people how to hold on to hope, you're going to have to tell real stories that glow in the dark."

Sebastian looks across the Rue de Dunkerque. When he turns back they are gone. He feels the air growing cooler and can hear the night sounds rise.

Kalyn McCall

King Kong (1933)

King Kong (1933) is my favorite film. I've seen every remake and sequel, but the original still holds my heart. But why? It tells the story of Denham as he embarks to Skull Island to make a motion picture. After plucking a down-on-her-luck actress named Ann Darrow from the streets of Depression-era NYC, they sail to the legendary island, only to come face-to-face with Kong, a fifty-foot gorilla. Awed by Darrow, Kong kidnaps the "golden woman," setting him on his path of inevitable destruction. Once in civilization, he must be brought down after snatching Darrow and taking her atop the Empire State Building. Planes attack, he falls to his death, and Denham remarks, "'Twas beauty that killed the beast."

From a cinematic standpoint, *King Kong* is a titan, an unquestionably significant entry in the development of American film. *Kong* is the godfather of *Jurassic Park* and *Alien*. It directly inspired Japan's *Godzilla*, kicking off the kaiju craze. Technologically, the classic showcased game-changing innovation and achievement. It employed the use of miniatures, rear-projected backgrounds, painstaking stop-motion animation, mobile camerawork, and dynamic sound design, enabling the world of *Kong* to come alive. Over 80 years later, the film's influence is still felt.

However, the film is often discussed as a parable of twentieth-century racism and racial fears, particularly those of miscegenation and Black barbarism. While its creators stated the film was a modern interpretation of beauty and the beast, *King Kong* relies heavily on racist tropes, themes, and imagery commonplace at the time. In the age of Jim Crow and scientific racism, Black people were depicted as savages, ape-like beasts, and monsters to be conquered. Texts like Thomas Dixon's *The Clansman* and the film it inspired, *The Birth of a Nation* (1915), relied on these tropes to justify and reaffirm White dominion. In *Kong*, a Black monster falls in love with a White captive, evoking themes of colonialism and slavery. Journeying to Skull Island, Denham remarks that there is something there that no White man has seen before. Upon arrival, they come across Black primitives worshiping Kong in a ceremony. Once the tribe sees Ann, the chief offers 6 Black women for her, suggesting they are worth less. Returning to America, Kong is put in chains, taught fear, and forced across the ocean for economic exploitation. In the final act, as a chained Kong stands aloft on a Broadway stage, Denham boasts, "He was the king and the god of the world he knew. Now he comes to civilization, merely captive, a show to gratify your curiosity." As a Black woman, why would I like this movie?

To complicate things further, some see *King Kong* as a metaphor for the trials of Joe Louis, one of the greatest boxers of all time. Louis dominated the ring at a time when Black people were supposed to be inferior. So furious were people with his success, and his tendency to date outside his race, that in 1910 Jim Jeffries, the Great White Hope, came out of retirement to bring him down. Reportedly, Jeffries stated his intention of returning to the ring was to "demonstrate that a White man is king of them all." Jeffries lost, and race riots swept the nation. But in *Kong*, the beast is taken out.

The thing is when I think of *Kong*, I think of my dad, who grew up in Jim Crow South Carolina. Since I was little, whenever there was a monster marathon on tv, he and I were glued to the screen. We've seen every *Kong* iteration, every entry in the *Godzilla* franchise, and all the knockoffs they've inspired. No matter how old I've gotten, each time a new film is released – including this year's *Godzilla vs. King Kong* (2021) – we refrain from watching it until we can together. After watching *Kong: Skull Island* (2017), I was inspired to ask him, "Do you remember the first time you went to the movies?" He did, but his answer took me aback. He discussed the first time his schoolteacher in Florence took him and his friends to a theater, and the excitement he felt as he walked up to his seat on the balcony. "At the time, it was the norm," he said. "There was no anger, no disappointment.

In Florence, we knew we were Black and we were supposed to walk up the stairs. . . There was nothing traumatic until the first time we didn't go upstairs. Then we realized what we were missing." I knew that there was a time when theaters were segregated, but it's another thing to realize that was the world he knew. And yet for him, it was a happy memory because it was in that balcony that he saw his first movie, a monster movie, one of the many inspired by *King Kong*. Eventually, he saw *Kong* there too. At a time when he, a Black boy, was supposed to be afraid, these films brought him joy. That's why he loved them so much and that's why he watches them – they are something he felt worth sharing with me so I could feel that joy too.

Kong is a simple film with a complicated legacy. On the one hand, it's an enthralling epic that defined American film culture. On the other, it's a relic of America's dark past. To me, it's everything, because Kong is the story's true hero. On-screen, he is a tragic, sympathetic figure. The film's racial worldviews further accentuate his innocence, as he did nothing wrong but exist freely in a world that expected submission. Off-screen, he is still the god and the king of the world he created. The power of his character not only launched a genre but ensured that despite his death, he could not be defeated.

Moreover, despite *Kong*'s racist elements, time has shown that chains will break, and fear will be overcome. There are many films like *King Kong* that can cause one to pause. How do we reconcile that one person's pleasure is another's pain? Can a film like *King Kong* be both problematic and a beloved classic? Perhaps we can find peace through context and conversation. It's okay to enjoy a film while critiquing it, coming face-to-face with the uncomfortable realities that shaped our past. It's okay especially when we know that complex past does not have to be our future. Thinking of how far my dad has come from that segregated theater, how much the world has changed, and that he was able to share the film with me in a new

178

world, I am at peace knowing that no chains could hold Kong down. Kong is king and always has been.

Scott Silsbe

**Flights of Angels: Scattered Notes on a Personal History
with *Wings of Desire***

"Perhaps we are *here* in order to say: house,
bridge, fountain, gate, pitcher, fruit-tree, window—
at most: column, tower…but to *say* them, you must understand,
to say them *more* intensely than the things themselves
ever dreamed of existing."
—Rainer Maria Rilke (trans. Stephen Mitchell), "The Ninth Elegy,"
Duino Elegies

    Time and memory, memory and time. I think it was in
the spring or summer of 1995 that I, age 17, took a job at the
Blockbuster Video on West Road in Woodhaven, my
"Downriver" suburb south of Detroit. I had to contribute a
lock of my long hair to get the job so the Blockbuster higher-
ups could be assured I wasn't a pothead. I wasn't necessarily
a film-buff at age 17, though I remember movies being a
vivid part of my life for about as far back as I can access my
memory. I can recall with relative clarity seeing *Snow White
and the Seven Dwarfs* (1937) and *Return of the Jedi* (1983) in the
theater as a child. And I can think of specific memories of
viewing movies at home—watching Altman's *Popeye* (1980)
with my father or watching *The Naked Gun* (1988) with my
childhood buddy, Josh.

    What possessed me to apply at Blockbuster, I don't
quite remember now. It could be there just weren't that many
employment opportunities for me at that time. I do know
that I was excited that one of the few perks of the job—
besides a complimentary 20-ounce Coca-Cola per shift—was
5 free VHS rentals a week. This allowed me to rewatch old
favorites, check out new releases, and explore movies from
the past that I'd never seen before. One section of the store
that intrigued me was the one holding foreign films. I'm not
sure about this now, but I want to say the placard over these
shelves just read, "FOREIGN." The movies there in the
"Foreign" section certainly were foreign to me. I don't

remember watching any films with subtitles as a child or in my early teen years.

A quick aside about the Blockbuster Video... it's likely influenced by a vintaged, nearly 30-year-old nostalgia, but thinking about it now, there was a bit of a magic to the place. Okay, it's just a suburban chain video store. But like the record stores I used to frequent in Dearborn, and the coffeeshops of Wyandotte or Livonia, there seemed to me to be a cultural significance to it. Growing up in the suburbs with a teenage interest in the arts (I probably would not have used the phrase "the arts" then), I developed a sort of ravenous appetite for discovering and learning about new-to-me things of a sort. At the record stores, I found albums I hadn't heard before that changed my ideas about music. At the coffeeshops, I met other people who liked to talk about books and records. And at the Blockbuster, I recall having discussions about music and movies with coworkers, my fellow VHS-tape-slingers. I remember bonding with a coworker named Paul over the new-to-video movie *Clerks* (1994). Paul had a laser-disc player — newer technology then — and he was able to 'dub' me a VHS tape of his *Clerks* laserdisc that had bonus footage, including the original ending.

It was also around this time that I found the Main Art Theater in Royal Oak. Royal Oak was about a half hour drive due north of Woodhaven, just up over on the other side of downtown Detroit. The Main was the first "art theater" that I knew of. One of the first films I think I saw there was Todd Solondz's *Welcome to the Dollhouse* (1995). But it wasn't the last. Other films I believe I saw at the Main Art — *I Shot Andy Warhol* (1996), *Trainspotting* (1997), *Washington Square* (1997), and *Run Lola Run* (1998).

I don't remember when I first saw Wim Wenders's *Wings of Desire* (1987) and I'm not positive I got it from my Blockbuster on West Road, but I *think* I did. I think it must have been some years later — my college years. I would return home from Kalamazoo to visit my hometown girlfriend, Cortney — she and I had met as coworkers there at the

Blockbuster. And sometimes, we would return to our old workplace for a VHS rental. At school, my studies were focused on literature, philosophy, creative writing, and German language. So, upon reflection, *Wings of Desire* was a perfect prescription for my interests.

The film opens—even before the title sequence—with a black-and-white shot of a pen writing on a page and a disembodied voice speaking in German, saying, "Als das Kind kind war…" In translation, the first line of the film is, "When the child was a child, it walked with its arms swinging." The voice speaking—I believe it's that of actor Bruno Ganz—ends up saying some of these first lines in a sing-song, nursery rhyme kind of voice. This is the "Song of Childhood," written by poet Peter Handke. I'll get to Handke a little later. After the pen writes out the "Song of Childhood," then come the titles.

As the words *Wings of Desire* fade from the screen, we're shown a shot (still in monochrome) of the sun through clouds, followed by a close-up of a human eye opening. This is followed by an aerial shot moving over streets and apartment buildings of Berlin, the camera working as the eye of an angel. This, in turn, transitions to a shot of Bruno Ganz as a winged angel looking down from the broken spire of the Kaiser Wilhelm Gedächtniskirche. A child walking through a crosswalk down below notices him and stops in the middle of the street looking up at him. Another child on a bus sees him, too, nudging her sister, saying, "Look." All the while, the minimal score of Jürgen Knieper plays.

A murmur of indistinguishable human voices. Another close-up—this time of an angel's wing flapping. And then the angel-eye camera descends to street level. Once it does this, we are able to discern the inner thoughts of individual Berliners. A man walking down the street with a baby strapped to his back thinking, "The delight of lifting one's head out here in the open, of seeing the colors in all men's eyes, enlightened by the sun." A shot of a bird soaring overhead. A woman on a bicycle (also with a child in tow) thinking, "At last mad, no longer alone. At last mad, at last redeemed. At last mad, at last at peace." A shot of an airplane in the sky. We're four minutes in.

Rewatching the film now in 2022, I can figure that it was not quite like any film I had seen when I first saw it back in the '90s. Sure, I had seen what I had considered "art films" at the theater in Royal Oak. But there was something different here. I don't know exactly how I would have articulated it then. But watching it now, what seems clear to me is that Wenders begins the film with a trust in images and the lyricality of language and he lets them guide the film. We the viewer tag along with two angels—first Bruno Ganz portraying Damiel, then later his buddy, Cassiel (played by Otto Sander)—and much of the first hour of the film is following the angels as they observe humans and listen in on their thoughts. Upon my first viewing, I might have said the movie was "slow," indicating that it wasn't concerned with rushing the plot or storyline along. Roger Ebert notes this kind of idea in his review of the film—"[The movie] moves slowly, but you don't grow impatient because there is no plot to speak of and so you don't fret that it should move to its next predictable stage. It is about being, not doing." A plot *does* eventually come together in the film. But I can remember how exciting my first viewing or two was for me, how I could feel *Wings of Desire* changing my perception of what movies could do and how they could do it.

Wings of Desire was, in his own words, a 'homecoming movie' for director Wim Wenders. In the 2003 documentary, *The Angels Among Us*, Wenders explains, "I'd lived in America for 8 years. I'd come back. And I tried to rediscover this country of mine through the city of Berlin, which was my favorite place in Germany." For Wenders, the filming of *Wings of Desire* was an exploration of Berlin. But it was also an attempt at capturing or documenting the state of that unique city at a unique time in its history. As film scholar Leigh Singer states in a piece called "5 Visual Themes in *Wings of Desire*," "Perhaps acknowledging the tradition of early 'city symphony' silent films like Dziga Vertov's *Man with a Movie Camera* (1929) or even Walter Ruttmann's *Berlin,*

Symphony of a City (1927), *Wings of Desire* is also in part a wonderful time capsule of wintry, pre-unification Berlin." Of course, Wenders could not have known that The Wall would fall just two years after the release of his film.

Though the inspiration for the idea of using the angels in the film came from multiple sources, an early influence was the poetry of Rainer Maria Rilke. Wenders had been reading Rilke's poems daily at the time. Rilke was fond of using angels in his poems and they are especially present in his *Duino Elegies*. Wenders saw the angels as a good premise for being able to capture all of the ins and outs of the city of Berlin. Wenders again, from *The Angels Among Us* doc— "They could really be everywhere and appear everywhere. They could cross through walls, could of course also cross through *The* Wall, they could be omnipresent, and they would allow me to have this complete overview of the city…They should be invisible…Then the idea popped up that they might even be able to listen to our thoughts, which would allow me to use a lot of interior voice and stuff and talk about things that normally people wouldn't talk about, that they would only think about."

Perhaps this is true of the creation of all films, but there was a great collaborative spirit involved in the making of *Wings of Desire*. For one thing, early on Wenders enlisted the help of his previous collaborator, Peter Handke. With the basic concept of the mind-reading angels in Berlin (and not much more), Wenders traveled to Salzburg to visit Handke, with the idea to pitch him the idea and have Handke write or cowrite a screenplay for/with him. When Wenders pitched the idea to Handke, Handke liked the concept, but said he didn't know how to do it. However, the story idea stuck with Handke. Shortly after Wenders's visit, Handke wrote Wenders a letter. Handke in the *Angels Among Us* doc—"I told him, 'I can't tell you a story; I can't write you a story. You have to shoot the film and I will send you every day, during one month or so, what is crossing my mind or my soul.'" So Handke began writing a series of monologues and dialogues for Wenders to use for the film. It was Handke's idea for the angel Damiel to become human. It was Wenders's idea to have there be a love story.

Once Wenders had the Handke-penned monologues, he thought of them as 'islands' to leap from as a sort of narrative for the film. Wenders began making the film with no finished script. Handke on Wenders—"His force is creating atmosphere, creating room, space, for instance, and this is sometimes, for a movie, more touching than telling a straight-forward story." Wenders felt that he was in some ways unprepared, but he also felt there was a great flexibility in not having a set script. The collaboration of the improvised script extended to his actors as well. Bruno Ganz: "He had no script, no dialogue, nothing you usually have, the whole time we were somehow under construction...Mainly, it was really kind of brainstorming, and talking about how we got in touch with this world of angels." When Wenders approached Otto Sander with the concept for the film, according to Sander, it was just two sentences on a sheet of paper describing the angels in Berlin. Sander liked the idea, but asked Wenders, "But who will find the story?" And Wenders replied that they all would, together.

Another key contribution to the film was the cinematography of Henri Alekan. Wenders decided the film was to be shot primarily in black and white. Once he had that idea combined with the invisibility of the angels, he had his heart set on getting 80-year-old Alekan to come out of retirement to work on *Wings*... with him. And he was successful. One of Alekan's brilliant touches was to create the monochrome world of the angels with a special filter. Wenders—"He shot the whole film with one filter he had hand-made himself in the '30s with the silk stocking of his grandmother. And that material was impossible to find and we only had that one thing, fragile thing, and it was already 50 years old. And I had to get in front of the lens for every shot and it had to be attached very carefully because it of course didn't fit with the modern camera—the equipment had to be sort of taped in front of every lens." The switch to color to signify the view of humans has always been an

185

intriguing effect to me. The first nod that came to mind for me was the color transition in *The Wizard of Oz* (1939) once Dorothy opens the door to Oz. But as noted by several film scholars including Robert Philip Kolker and Peter Beicken, a more precise filmic reference is the Powell & Pressburger film *A Matter of Life and Death* (1946), where the monochrome represents the world of immortals vs. the full color of mortal existence.

Again thinking back on my initial viewing or two of *Wings of Desire,* I can understand some of the things that really moved me or that I found striking about the film. I have no doubt that I was taken with the idea of the angels living in (or at least regularly occupying) a library, the Staatsbibliothek zu Berlin. The university library of my undergrad years and the Kalamazoo Public Library (including its Friends of the Library Bookstore!) were certainly sacred spaces to me. And I liked the idea of angels hovering over my shoulder as I looked through the stacks at the seemingly endless number of tomes to pull from or as I sat with them piled up around me at a library table.

One scene that I know was important to me was the scene early on in the film featuring Damiel and Cassiel sitting in a convertible in a car showroom. Cassiel pulls out a small notebook and lists historical events of the day then moves on to small happenings of note that he had witnessed so far. "And today...on the Lilienthaler Chaussee," he says, "a man slowed down and looked over his shoulder into space. And a man who wanted to end it all today put a different collector's stamp on each farewell letter. Then he spoke English with an American soldier for the first time since his schooldays—and quite fluently." He goes on. He then asks Damiel, "And what have you to report?" Damiel returns the favor, taking out his own notebook and telling Cassiel of his daily observations. I like how these angels are documenting, are recording events, are "preserving the past," like how Wenders was preserving Berlin history with his film.

The convertible conversation turns from the two angels sharing their observations to Damiel's expressing his discontent with his life as an immortal, articulating his desire to take part in the sensual experiences of human life. "To have a fever," Damiel says to Cassiel, "or get your fingers black from the newspaper, to be excited not just by the mind but by a meal, the curve of a neck, an ear…to feel your bones as you walk along." I think this convertible scene meant so much to me at the time because it reminded me of the poetry I was reading at the time and the things I was learning from that poetry. The work that the angels did to capture small, beautiful moments—that was what I wanted to do with my poems. And the way Damiel viewed human life—his envious view of what we get to experience—it made me think of Whitman and his celebration of himself, his body, his humanity.

Like all great art, *Wings of Desire* rewards upon revisiting. It feels to me like there are endless things to discover, appreciate, and discuss about the film. One thing that strikes me as particularly interesting now is the way it seems like the majority of the inner thoughts that the angels eavesdrop on concern the loneliness or anxieties that the humans feel. In some instances, the angels are able to provide some comfort to those struggling. A scene that resonates strongly with me now is when Damiel is comforting a victim of a roadside accident.

A man appears to have been knocked off his motorcycle by a car. His overheard thoughts reveal his fear that he is dying. Damiel approaches him, putting his hands on the man's head, and soothes the man by speaking what sounds like a poem—"As I came up the mountain, out of the misty valley into the sun, the fire on the cattle range, the potatoes in the ashes, the boathouse floating far out on the lake. The Southern Cross…" The man stops thinking his anxious thoughts. And he begins to say the same words as Damiel—"The Far East. High up north. The Wild West. The Great Bear Lake." Damiel stops, but the man continues without him, saying, "Tristan da Cunha Island. The Mississippi Delta. Stromboli. The old houses of Charlottenburg. Albert Camus. The morning light. The eyes of a child. Swimming by the waterfall. The spots from the first drops of rain." Damiel walks away as the man continues.

One reason I find this scene so striking is simply because of its tenderness and vision. I like that the angel is able to comfort the motorcyclist with poetry. But another reason I find it so meaningful is that I feel it is a beautiful capture of what it is to be an artist. To me, an essential part of the artistic process is inspiration from outside sources—and namely, significantly, other artists. In that way, all art is collaboration. Damiel's transference of his poem to the motorcyclist and the motorcyclist's continuation of the poem mimics the collaboration between Wenders and Handke on the *Wings of Desire* film, but more than that, it is a representation of the great genealogy of inspiration we can trace in all artistic output.

I didn't even get to the love story. Or the old man Homer character. Or Peter Falk. I didn't talk about Nick Cave and the Bad Seeds and I only briefly touched on the inventive score by Jürgen Knieper. As I said, there's a lot that can be discussed. What I always felt was most rewarding about *Wings of Desire* was how it made me feel a renewed appreciation and passion for human life, for living, for experience. And how it made me see new ways that a piece of art can instruct, inspire, and comfort. What moves me about the film now is how it portrays how trying human life is—how full of loneliness and anxiety and hopelessness it can feel—and yet how full of beauty and wonder it also is. Thanks to the thrill and joy of discovery—in learning, in knowledge. At the end of the film, the pen writes on the page, "I know now what no angel knows." Perhaps we are here in order to discover and learn and know those kinds of things. To again and again address the world, saying, "Now I'm starting to understand." To feel repeatedly that we have just arrived or that we have embarked.

Alexa Weik

My Favorite Film

As someone who has written dozens of scripts, produced movies and TV shows, and worked for the past decade or so as a film scholar, I often get asked about my favorite film.

My problem is I don't have one. Not really.

That appears to be an unsatisfactory answer for those who would like to know. Given my background and the thousands and thousands of films to choose from, surely, I must have a favorite?

I have been asking myself this question. A lot. And I have come up with some answers—mostly-true answers for myself, and more appropriate ones I feel comfortable voicing in public. Naturally, both types of answers have changed with age, perspective, and profession.

As a teenager, living in Germany in the 1980s, I didn't have one favorite film, I had lots of them, and they were all about love in one way or another. When prompted, I would recite scenes, sequences, or entire films freely from memory. You could literally have woken me up at 3 am, and I would have been able to produce any dialogue from any moment of Howard Hawks's *Bringing Up Baby*. Not the original dialogue, mind you, but the German words of the dubbed version, which aired every three weeks or so on public television. It was quite disorienting when, a few years ago, I finally got around to watching Hawks's original film because I was teaching it in a class on the American screwball comedy, and Hepburn and Grant got all their best lines wrong. In such moments of cinematic confusion, it is imperative to carry on as if nothing was the matter, but I couldn't help providing the correct translations throughout the entire screening, my lips forming silent German words. I cannot stand dubbing nowadays, but it's what I grew up with, and *Bringing Up Baby* might be the only film in which I actually *prefer* the punchlines in German.

189

I could add other Hollywood classics—*Arsenic and Old Lace, Breakfast at Tiffany's, What's Up, Doc?*—that were almost as high on my list. But I will admit there were others, quite a lot of them, that did not necessarily match the quality of Hawks's masterpiece, and yet I developed the same kind of mastery memorizing them once I got a little older. *9 ½ Weeks, Tequila Sunrise,* and *Dirty Dancing* were among them, as were lesser-known films such as *Thief of Hearts,* which helped me develop an unhealthy addiction to Häagen-Dazs ice cream (Rum Raisin, for the insiders, if there are any left). Some of these favorites are best remembered fondly and never to be watched again. I made that mistake with *Tequila Sunrise,* and all I can say in its favor is: Michelle Pfeiffer is in it.

Which brings me to the 90s, when I was working in television and developing a whole new perspective on what it means to create and produce a film. I started reading scripts and later turned to writing them myself, churning out over 160 episodes of a German TV show. My favorite film of this era, without a doubt, is Martin Scorsese's *The Age of Innocence.* But there were others: *Reality Bites, High Fidelity, Before Sunrise, Boyz n the Hood, Smoke Signals,* and *Good Will Hunting,* to name just a few. This is where I must admit that a great many films are categorically excluded from my consideration because they belong to genres that, with very few exceptions, I don't watch. Horror would be one, war films another, except for those that are anti. Most psycho-thrillers, too, unless I can arrange myself with not being able to sleep for a few weeks afterward. I did watch *Silence of the Lambs,* but it will never come anywhere near my non-existent top ten. It should also be noted that this list bends heavily toward American films with a few German (*Goodbye Lenin*), British (*The Full Monty*), and French (*Le grand bleu*) exceptions. As a friend of mine has put it pointedly, I'm surprisingly limited in my tastes, so how can I even be expected to have a proper favorite film?

Once we get to the 2000s, me being a PhD student in San Diego at the time, there are a few independent comedies that come to mind—*Sideways, Juno, Little Miss Sunshine*—and so many more recent films could be added, from Damien Chazelle's *Whiplash* and Tom McCarthy's *Spotlight* to Theodore Melfi's *Hidden Figures* and Benh Zeitlin's *Beasts of the Southern Wild*. When I started working on film as an ecocritical scholar my interest shifted toward the analytical and, for the first time in my life, toward nonfiction. By now I've watched hundreds of eco-documentaries and learned so much from them about the perilous state of our world and engaged filmmaking. There are dozens of films I appreciate for what they try to achieve, and I have written about many of them. But I would be hard pressed to name a favorite. As a scholar, I no longer think about favorites much. I think about what is interesting and worth exploring. And luckily, the list of such films is long and ever-expanding.

Which begs the question, of course: what's my favorite film?

If I were in a situation in which my life or something equally irreplaceable depended on my answer, I would say Ridley Scott's *Blade Runner*. First, because it is an appropriate and safe choice for a film scholar and Americanist, and that's the kind of choice you would want in such a situation. And second, because it's probably true. *Blade Runner* has everything I love in a film, something to admire, something to think about, something to talk about, and something to feel very deeply.

And of course, it's a love story, isn't it? Apparently, some things never change.

Kyle Woodruff

Friend of Scarecrow

Tragically, Sigmund Freud died less than a month after *The Wizard of Oz* was released in theaters. Had he lived long enough to study the film's impact on the world, he would have formulated an entirely new complex: The Scarecrow Complex. Further, I believe that he would have pointed to me as patient zero for this very real, very serious condition that definitely exists.

What is The Scarecrow Complex, you ask? Much like the similarly named Oedipal, Electra, and Military-Industrial Complexes, The Scarecrow Complex is a psychoanalyses condition that develops during childhood. As with the other three complexes, The Scarecrow Complex involves an intense subconscious attraction to an early childhood figure that informs a person's sexual proclivities into adulthood. With the Oedipal and Electra complexes, the objects of subconscious attraction are the mother and father, respectively; with the Military-Industrial Complex, the object of subconscious attraction is the Raytheon AGM-65 Maverick surface to air missile; and with The Scarecrow Complex, the object of subconscious attraction is the Scarecrow as portrayed by actor Ray Bolger in the 1939 musical classic *The Wizard of Oz*.

All of my celebrity crushes are based on this deep, subconscious attraction to Ray Bolger's iteration of the Scarecrow (not Ray Bolger himself, but rather Ray Bolger AS the Scarecrow). They all possess some combination of physical and personality traits also modeled by the Scarecrow. Actor Zachary Levi for instance, has the Scarecrow's lanky build and bumbling personality (prior to bulking up for Shazam anyway); Paul Newman, with eyes as blue as the Kansas sky, shares the Scarecrow's prominent painted nose and proclivity for creamy salad dressings (Paul Newman's nose is famously always painted brown in every role, you do not need to look this up); Dick Van Dyke shares

192

the Scarecrow's talent for singing, dancing, and taking roles where he talks to birds; Sean Connery has a funny voice and a drinking problem (how else can you explain the Scarecrow's wobbly walk?); Marlon Brando has forehead wrinkles begging to be covered in burlap; Gene Kelly is a short athletic dancer with an affinity for apples; Jack Nicholson's iconic eyebrows, clearly inspired by the scarecrows triangular points; Cary Grant's sexy display of overconfidence that makes me believe that he too would confuse an isosceles triangle and a right triangle when reciting Pythagorean's theorem – the list goes on and on. Even in real life, everyone I've dated, from the Mormon, the death metal singer, Bryce (he was pretty brainless), the engineer, and the comedian, fit the Scarecrow mold.

The most Scarecrow of them all, however, is my all-time crushiest celebrity crush: Harrison Ford. "Harrison Ford?" you ask. "Why, he's the least Scarecrow out of all your picks!" Well, hear me out. Harrison Ford, in the popular image, inhabits a certain kind of midwestern stoicism. He comes off as a man of the land, an unflappable constant. Even when he plays a robot detective from the future who doesn't know he is a robot, he seems more like an annoyed dad from Indiana. Well, what could be more midwestern, stoic, and of the land than a man made of straw who stands in a field and lets crows pick at his face? I can't think of anything, and neither can you. The only thing that could make Harrison Ford more Scarecrow would be if he were literally made of straw. But hey, a girl can dream.

Biographies

Jeffrey Alfier's most recent book of poetry, *The Shadow Field*, was published by Louisiana Literature Press (2020).

Tobi Alfier has published in literary journals such as *War, Literature and the Arts*, *The American Journal of Poetry*, *Washington Square Review*, *The Ogham Stone*, *Permafrost*, and *Gargoyle*.

Dibakar Barua is a retired English professor and an indolent writer. His poems, short stories, and essays have appeared in various literary magazines.

Joan E. Bauer is the author of two poetry collections, *The Almost Sound of Drowning* (Main Street Rag, 2008) and *The Camera Artist* (Turning Point, 2021), and her new volume, *Fig Season*, is forthcoming from Turning Point in 2023.

Charlie Brice is the winner of the 2020 Field Guide Magazine Poetry Contest and is the author of *Flashcuts Out of Chaos* (2016), *Mnemosyne's Hand* (2018), *An Accident of Blood* (2019), and *The Broad Grin of Eternity* (2021), all from WordTech Editions.

Kelsey Bryan-Zwick's poetry collection, *Here Go the Knives* (Moon Tide Press) focuses on their decades surviving with debilitating scoliosis. Kelsey is a UC Santa Cruz alum and they've been twice nominated for both the Pushcart Prize and Best of the Net.

T. Anders Carson has published 5 books of poetry, the latest *Unfortunately, Thanks for Everything* by Pelekinesis Press, and has had his poems appear in 37 countries.

Douglas Cole has published six poetry collections and the novel *The White Field*, winner of the American Fiction Award.

Stephen Cooper, CSULB Professor of English, is editor, author, and writer-producer respectively of *Perspectives on John Huston*, *Full of Life: A Biography of John Fante*, and the Netflix Original Documentary *Struggle: The Life and Lost Art of Szukalski*.

Emily Elbom lives in Oregon and teaches various writing courses at Oregon State University, and she is a member of *Calyx Literary Journal's* editorial collective for both prose and poetry.

Gilad Elbom is the fiction editor of the North Dakota Quarterly; his first novel, *Scream Queens of the Dead Sea*, was published by Thunder's Mouth Press in 2004, and *Textual Rivalries: Jesus, Midrash, and Kabbalah*, was published by Fortress Press in 2022.

Kimberly Esslinger's poetry has appeared in publications such as *Spillway*, *Chiron Review*, and *Thrush*, and she recently completed her MFA in Poetry at CSULB.

Edward Field's books include *After the Fall: Poems Old and New*, *Magic Words: Poems*, *Variety Photoplays*, and *Stand Up, Friend, With Me*, and he has won various prestigious awards, including the Lamont Award from the Academy of American Poets and the Shelley Memorial Award from the Poetry Society of America.

Kate Flannery is an Editor-at-Large for *The Journal of Radical Wonder*, and her essays, poetry and fiction have been published in *Chiron Review*, *Shark Reef*, and *Ekphrastic Review*, as well as other literary journals.

Celeste Gainey is the author of the poetry collection *Gaffer*, and is the first woman to be admitted to the International Alliance of Theatrical Stage Employees (IATSE) as a gaffer.

Suzanne Greenberg is the author of, among other books, *Speed-Walk and Other Stories*, which won the Drue Heinz Literature Prize, *Lesson Plans*, and (as co-author with Lisa Glatt), the children's novels, *Abigail Iris: The One and Only* and *Abigail Iris: The Pet Project*.

George Hammons is a Southern California poet who writes about social justice, family, and love, and whose collection, *Witness*, was released by Picture Show Press in 2020.

Brian Harman received his MFA in creative writing from Cal State University, Long Beach, and his recent book, *Suddenly, All Hell Broke Loose!!!*, was published by Picture Show Press.

Donna Hilbert's latest book is *Threnody*, from Moon Tide Press, 2022, and she leads private workshops in Southern California

Paul Hostovsky's latest book is *Deaf & Blind* (Main Street Rag, 2020), and he has won a Pushcart Prize, two Best of the Net awards, and the FutureCycle Poetry Book Prize.

Kendall Johnson's stories and poems have appeared in such publications as *MacQueen's Quinterly*, *Tears in the Fence*, and *Litro*, and several books, and he is contributing editor to the *Journal of Radical Wonder*.

Serena Kamlani has a BA in Creative Writing from Sonoma State University and enjoys participating in yearly MFA seminars at Sarah Lawrence College.

Kalyn McCall is a historian of California, the West, and Black American history and culture. In addition to graduating from Stanford University and pursuing graduate studies at Harvard University, Kalyn enjoys researching local histories, working with students, and spending time with her dogs.

Bill Mohr's book *Holdouts: The Los Angeles Poetry Renaissance 1948-1992*, was published by the University of Iowa in 2011, and he has taught 20th century American literature and creative writing at California State University, Long Beach since 2006.

Dave Newman is the author of several books, including *Raymond Carver Will Not Raise Our Children*, *The Slaughterhouse Poems*, and *The Same Dead Songs*, and, in 2004, he received the Andre Dubus Novella Award.

Sarah M. Perna works on the long running daytime drama *The Bold and the Beautiful*, and has recently written two episodes for the show.

Benjamin Rosenbush is a singer-songwriter whose forthcoming debut book will be published by *Chiron Review Press* in 2023.

Patty Seyburn has published five collections of poems, including *Threshold Delivery* (Finishing Line Press, 2019), *Perfecta* (What Books Press, Glass Table Collective, 2014), and, *Hilarity*, which won the Green Rose Prize.

Faith Shearin is the author of seven books of poetry, including: *The Owl Question* (May Swenson Award), *Darwin's Daughter* (SFA University Press) and *Lost Language* (Press 53), and she has received awards from Yaddo, The National Endowment for the Arts, and The Barbara Deming Memorial Fund.

Scott Silsbe is the author of the books *Unattended Fire*, *The River Underneath the City*, *Muskrat Friday Dinner*, and *Meet Me Where We Survive*, and he is an assistant editor at Low Ghost Press.

Clifton Snider was a Long Beach-based poet whose books included *Stubborn Heart, The Plymouth Papers, Wrestling With Angels: A Tale of Two Brothers*, and *The Beatle Bump.*

Kareem Tayyar's books include *Keats in San Francisco & Other Poems* (Lily Poetry Review) and *The Prince of Orange County* (Pelekinesis), the latter of which received the 2020 Eric Hoffer Award for Young Adult Fiction.

Thomas R. Thomas publishes the small press Arroyo Seco Press, and his books include *The Art of Invisibility, Star Chasing, Three on a Wire*, and *Missing Shaun.*

Brian Walter's essays and fiction have appeared in (among others) *Boulevard, The Santa Monica Review, Cineaction*, and *North Dakota Quarterly.*

Kyle Woodruff is a graduate of UCI, and a middle school teacher in Orange County, California.

Alexa Weik Von Mossner is a writer, professor, and ecocritical literary scholar whose books include *Affective Ecologies: Empathy, Emotion, and Environmental Narrative* (Ohio State University Press) and *Cosmopolitan Minds: Literature, Emotion, and the Transnational Imagination* (University of Texas Press).

Rafael Zepeda's books include *Desperados, Tao Driver and Selected Poems*, and *Horse Medicine and Other Stories*, and his awards include the National Endowment of the Arts Creative Writing Fellowship.

Acknowledgements

The editors would like to thank the literary journals where some of these works first appeared.

Other books by Arroyo Seco Press include:

The Fireflies Around Us by Kendall Johnson

Charcoal and Ink sketches and poetry by Ranney Campbell

The Litany of Missing by Aruni Wijesinghe

Moments From My Mother's Life by Judith Grammel Evans

Rejection Letters by Kevin Ridgeway

More Fireflies by Kendall Johnson

Fireflies Against Darkness by Kendall Johnson

I Know Not What I See by Alessandra C. Park

SurvivalEye by Mare Heron Hake

Let Us Now Praise Ordinary Things by Kareem Tayyar

Once It's Over by Lloyd David Aquino

Building Stonehenge by Marc Maurus

In the Muddle of the Night by Betsy Mars & Alan Walowitz

Pimp by Ranney Campbell

Fossil of the New Scene by Kevin Ridgeway

Noir Librarian by Marilyn N. Robertson

What I Didn't Say by James Mauch

Seven Countries by Various Authors

Chapbooks

Crossroads of Stars And White Lightning by Larry Raymond Duncan

My Favorite Mistake by Shannon Phillips

Seaglass by Elder Zamora

On the Burning Shore by Kevin Ridgeway

Striking Distance by Tere Sievers

The Old Masters by Jeffrey Graessley

Gymlationship by K. Andrew Turner

Fruit of the Dead by Francesca Terzano

Transitory Myth by Sarah Elizabeth Miller

Good Girl by Lorraine Biteranta

Midnight in Qatar by Lee Anne McIlroy

Life is But a Dream by Barbara Eknoian

Hungry to Bed by George Hammons

Stillness by Francesca Borella

Seventeen Poems Not About a Lover by Sarah Thursday

Whiskey Letters by Susan Vannatta

It Isn't That They Mean to Kill You by Penelope Moffet

Voyage by Sarah E. Gurney

No One Saves You by Kitty Anarchy

Holy Jim and Other Trails by Terry Wilhelm

Cauldron of Hisses by Penelope Moffet

Blue Book Chapbooks Series

Blue Book 1

Laughing in the Face of Death by Kevin Ridgeway

Days of Recent Divorce by John Brantingham

Northwest Passages by Kate Flannery

Grove Work by Kendall Johnson

Yes. Done. by Steven Schreiner & Ranney Campbell

Blue Book 2

Caddish by Ranney Campbell

Mercy by Kevin D LeMaster

Evening of the Peyote Flower by Zack Nelson-Lopiccolo

Soul by S. J. Perry

Bedside Manners by Aruni Wijesinghe

www.ingramcontent.com/pod-product-compliance
Lightning Source LLC
Chambersburg PA
CBHW060216180626
46813CB00007B/2849